GREENWICH KILLING TIME

Kinky Friedman, former leader of the band The Texas Jewboys, lives on a ranch in the Texas Hill Country with six dogs, two cats and one armadillo. He is the author of fourteen and a half internationally acclaimed mystery novels and nine country music albums. These days, he travels the world, singing the songs that made him infamous and reading from the books that made him respectable.

*by the same author*

A CASE OF LONE STAR
WHEN THE CAT'S AWAY
FREQUENT FLYER
MUSICAL CHAIRS
ELVIS, JESUS AND COCA-COLA
ARMADILLOS AND OLD LACE
GOD BLESS JOHN WAYNE
THE LOVE SONG OF J. EDGAR HOOVER
ROADKILL
BLAST FROM THE PAST
SPANKING WATSON
THE MILE HIGH CLUB

KINKY FRIEDMAN

# Greenwich Killing Time

Vandam Press
New York, Kerrville, Jerusalem, Honolulu

This Vandam Press book contains the complete text of the original hardcover edition. This book also contains a new introduction by the author.

GREENWICH KILLING TIME

A Vandam Press book published by arrangement with the author.

Printing History
This book was first published by
William Morrow and Company in 1986



First Vandam Press printing: August, 2000



The Vandam Press, Inc., website is at:
http://www.vandampress.com

ISBN: 0-9702383-0-4

Vandam Press books are published by Vandam Press, Inc.
The name 'Vandam Press' and the stylized 'V' logo used by
Vandam Press, Inc., are registered trademarks.

2 4 6 8 10 9 7 5 3 1

To Min

ACKNOWLEDGMENTS

The author would like to thank the following people for their help and encouragement: Tom Friedman, Larry Sloman, Don Imus, Marice Friedman and Ted Mann; Esther Newberg at ICM; James Landis and Jane Meara at Beech Tree Books; and Steven Rambam, technical adviser.

The author would also like to thank Michael R. McGovern for the use of his mother's Smith-Corona typewriter.

Robert B. Parker once told me: 'When they start saying they admire your earlier work, that's when you know you've arrived.' He also once said: 'Anyone who dots their 'I's with a Star of David can't be all bad.' I agree with both sentiments. That's part of the reason I'm so excited and honored that such a well-respected, prestigious publishing house as Vandam Press has chosen my first five books to inaugurate their new Masters of Crime series. They could've chosen the Five Books of Moses but mine have been out of print longer.

*Greenwich Killing Time* was the first book I ever wrote. I wrote it in 1984 and it was published in 1986. I was doing a lot of Peruvian marching powder at the time so I don't remember too much about writing it, but I do recall a couple of things. I borrowed the title from my friend Ted Mann. I borrowed the typewriter, an old Smith-Corona, from my friend, the future Village Irregular, Mike McGovern. Mike graciously loaned me the typewriter claiming he'd missed many important deadlines with the instrument. It had, I later learned, once belonged to his mother before she'd been bugled to Jesus years earlier. I took this as a sign of the Lord's hand at work in the world. It could've been, of course, just another case of a Jew borrowing a typewriter.

Though most of the books have been set in New York (with the exception of *Armadillos and Old Lace*, set in Texas, and the soon-to-be-published *Steppin' on a Rainbow*, set in Hawaii), *Greenwich Killing Time* is the only one that was written in New York. Some critics have remarked, not unkindly, we hope, that the book smells like New York. If this is true it is no doubt because of the truly visceral voyage one goes through in writing a first novel. It's almost as if your first novel writes you.

I'd been reading a lot of Georges Simenon at the time and Simenon believed that the best, most original work was often accomplished by beginning with nothing more than a street address written on the back of an envelope. The street address Simenon probably used was somewhere in Paris. In my case, I remember literally writing on the back of an envelope the words

'Yesterday Street'. It was a point of reference, a starting point. This left a hell of a lot to the imagination, to the ear, to the eye, and to what type of person you wanted to be when you grew up. It also meant that you would be writing with a ruthless economy of words in a voice reserved for a silent witness like a long-lost friend or a cat or a dead sweetheart.

Some say *Greenwich Killing Time* is my best book. I like to refer to those people as 'insects trapped in amber'. I believe that my best book is always the next one. I will give them this, however. A certain innocence seems to attach to some things after a while, whether or not it was there in the first place. Most of the characters that populate this book are real and most of the names I used are their real names. I didn't bother to change the names to protect the innocent because I did not think there was a hell of a lot of innocence to protect. On this point, however, I may have been wrong.

There is something to Nelson Algren's notion of 'achieved innocence'. It's an innocence you have to work for. It's never pure or guaranteed. But in time it may come to you, full of awkward grace, like a cat, or a long-lost friend, or a dead sweetheart from some forgotten address on yesterday street.

Kinky Friedman
August 14, 1999
Medina, Texas

# 1

I held the mescal up to the light and watched the worm slide across the bottom of the bottle. A gift from a friend just back from Mexico. The worm was fat and white and somewhat dangerous looking with great hallucinogenic properties attributed to it. You were supposed to eat it and it was supposed to make you so high you would need a stepladder to scratch your ass. We'd see.

I searched my wastebasket for a while till I located a dead, fairly well-preserved, half-smoked cigar and I fired it up. I remembered Winston Churchill's reputed words on the subject: 'They're gamier when resurrected.' Winston wasn't wrong.

I was leaning back in my chair, puffing a bit, just trying to keep the world at bay, when the phones rang. I was in the habit of keeping two red telephones at stage left and stage right of my desk, both connected to the same line. It sort of enhanced the importance of my calls and when they rang they burned right through you like a red-hot skewer. It was McGovern from the *Daily News*.

You had to like McGovern. He was a very friendly, very large half-Irish, half-Indian who, like every journalist I knew, would take a drink. He nevertheless had many charming and redeeming qualities, some of which were quite noticeably absent in the architecture of my personality. In fact, I often thought that between the two of us, we'd just about make up one fairly adequate human being.

'Get over here right away, man. This is serious. There's a body lying on the floor across the hall. Looks like a case for you.' He gave me an address on Jane Street fairly close by in the Village.

I didn't ask him a case of what? Riding up Hudson in the cab I reasoned that it wasn't the kind of case one would like to drink nor the kind one might possibly obtain from any recent unsavory sexualis.

I tipped the cabbie and got out at 42 Jane, opposite the only windmill in New York City, a weatherbeaten but proud remnant of long-ago Dutch masters. I climbed the steps and pushed the buzzer of Apartment 2B, where McGovern had lived since Christ was a cowboy, or at least since I'd known him.

As I cleared the second landing, I could see McGovern's huge form hovering above, displacing a great deal of the narrow hallway. 'Over here,' he whispered and led me across to the opposite end of the hall from his own place. 'In there,' he muttered.

I pushed the door open to Apartment 2E. There were several chairs pulled up around a table with a brightly checked red and white tablecloth. On the table was a plate of banana bread and another plate of Brie. There was a pitcher of Bloody Marys in which the ice was beginning to melt and several fairly nice crystal glasses.

One of the glasses was clearly smudged with bright pink lipstick, at least as clear as you could possibly get a smudge. It went with the decor because the man was holding a bouquet of long-stemmed pink roses. He was lying on the floor with a cute little hole right about where his third eye should be. The flowers he was holding were quite lovely but he definitely couldn't care less. On the floor beside the body was a little white card with the typewritten message: 'i'm sending you eleven roses . . . the twelfth rose is you.'

'There you have it,' said McGovern.

## 2

The cops from the Sixth Precinct came and went in a blue parade. There were a few plainclothesmen. McGovern was, by this time, across the hall on the blower to the *Daily News*.

The cops identified me about the same time they identified the stiff. Neither of us cut much ice with them. They remembered me from my first exploit two years before, which McGovern had written up lavishly in the *News*. The story had carried the gaudy headline: COUNTRY SINGER PLUCKS VICTIM FROM MUGGER.

Since that time I had evolved professionally from 'country singer' to 'Broadway composer' as I neared completion of my first musical comedy bound for the boards. But with several fortuitous forays into crime solving in the Village, I had also evolved into something between a gnat and a rather motheaten gadfly in the eyes of the officers of the Sixth Precinct.

'You . . . Stay there,' said the cop apparently in charge of the case, Detective Sergeant Buddy Fox. We'd met before. He was tall, lean, and mean, and he didn't like country music. He went through the pockets of the deceased. The assistant medical examiner arrived. The police photographer snapped away, kibbitzing with the print men who were dusting the articles on the table and with the assistant medical examiner, who occasionally chuckled and put his two cents in across the bland features of the face on the floor.

'What do you know about this?' Fox asked.

'Looks like a warning shot right between the eyes,' I said.

'See anyone?'

I shook my head.

'Hear the shot?' he asked.

Again I shook my head.

I won't tell you what he said next. A nicer version of it might read: 'Then what are you doing here, pal?'

It had worked so well I tried shaking my head a third time.

Detective Sergeant Fox became slightly agitato, but he controlled himself. Trembling only slightly, he impressed upon me the gravity of tampering with evidence in a homicide. His partner, Detective Sergeant Mort Cooperman, was shorter and a great deal stockier than Fox. He was breathing heavily. I wondered if he'd been out walking his pet stomach. He took down my address and phone number and then bellowed for me to bug out for the dugout. Actually, those were not his precise words, but that was the gist.

I left shaking my head, mostly for effect.

I took a cab back to 199B Vandam, cursed the absence of the freight elevator, and legged it up the four floors to my loft with the jungle of green plants and the sun-streaked southern exposure that made me the envy of many trendy, back-to-nature New Yorkers. Actually, the plants were there when I rented the place, but between thick incessant cigar smoke and my cat's constant chomping on them, we'd managed to make a dent or two in the foliage. About every six months or so I faithfully watered them whether they needed it or not.

I know the exact time because I have a small digital alarm clock, which I like to think of as a computer, and it keeps me on the cutting edge of the technological age. I log all incoming calls.

The phones rang at 8.23 p.m. It was McGovern.

'Good news and bad news,' he said. 'He had sublet the place for only about six months. His name is or was Frank Worthington, a part-time actor, part-time bartender, and apparently, a part-time bisexual. Or should I say a full-time bisexual?'

'Right.' I said.

'The bad news is where I'm calling from. I'm calling from the Sixth Precinct. They found the gun in my apartment.'

## 3

I wasted no time getting on the blower to my lawyer, Wolf Nachman. There are no good lawyers. There may be lady wrestlers and Catholic universities. There may be military intelligence. But a good lawyer is a contradiction in terms. When you needed one, you needed one, however, and I needed one. So Wolf was the one I called and he said he'd get right on it.

I brewed some coffee, lit a fresh cigar, and waited. It was a Friday night, the beginning of another fun-filled New York weekend in the Village for teenage hit-run drivers from New Jersey and assorted other Americans.

I turned on the twenty-four-hour all-news station. They had a slogan they kept repeating: 'You give us twenty-two minutes – we'll give you the world.' No deal, I thought.

They didn't have the story yet. At 11.53 p.m. the phones rang. I listened to Wolf howl at me for a while. He was moving heaven and earth but McGovern would probably be staying in the sneezer for at least the weekend. There was nothing to be done so I decided rather reluctantly to call it a night myself.

The cat yawned and stretched and I yawned and stretched and we both looked at each other. Sometimes I thought there wasn't a man, woman or child on this planet that I loved as much as that cat. What the cat was thinking was something else of course. I rarely meddled in the cat's personal affairs and she rarely meddled in mine. Neither of us was foolish enough to attribute human emotions to our pets.

The sounds of garbage trucks awakened me in the morning. Some people wake up to the sounds of church bells. Some people wake up to the sounds of birds. But in New York you wake up to the sounds of garbage trucks. Place is still filthy, of course. Can't have everything.

I brewed some strong black coffee and fed the cat. Then I walked the few blocks up to Sheridan Square to get a morning paper. That area is one of New York's throbbing nerve centers of drug-orientated, gay festivity at all hours of day and night. I liked to point out the area to tourists. General Sheridan's statue stands looking over the square but you can tell he isn't liking it much.

I bought a paper and glanced through it in a quaint Fourth Street restaurant that was about as big as my nose and was called The Bagel.

There was nothing. No flowers. No croaked bisexuals. No McGovern. Nary a by-line and nary a bi-line.

Strange.

I paid the check and hoofed it over to Jane Street, stopping only briefly at Village Cigars on Seventh Avenue for a few purchases for the household.

At 42 Jane Street the super was surly. He held a lingering, somewhat unfavorable impression of me from the old days when I used to crash with McGovern for months at a time. The only thing he seemed willing to give me was grief, so I left for a while and circled back, this time employing a set of keys I'd retained from way back when.

I tried one. It was rusty but it worked fine. Like a Haitian curse. I had it in mind to visit somebody on the third floor. I remembered her from a party about seven years ago. She was sort of an ingenue then. Couldn't wait to see her now. Seven years in New York is like a lifetime anywhere else.

I bounded up to the third floor. Carpet was getting a little threadbare up there. I'd have to mention it to the super. I knocked on the door of Apartment 3B, right above McGovern's. After some little cajoling and explaining, I was permitted entry into a dusty, dimly lighted apartment with enough drug paraphernalia to start a store in the East Village.

Adrian looked like a waxen insect.

'You look fine,' I lied.

'What do you want?' she said, motioning me with a weary gesture onto the couch next to her.

'I want to know about the guy that got croaked in Two-E. Bought any flowers lately, Adrian?' Sometimes the direct approach was the best.

Now she smiled a little. It wasn't a pleasant thing to see. She was well on her way to acquiring what is sometimes referred to as a 'New York face.' I think George Orwell was the one who said that by age fifty every man has the face he deserves. Orwell himself was only forty-seven when he died. Well, it can't be helped. But it goes ditto for women, to say the least. And it wasn't a particularly nice direction Adrian's face was taking. Something evil was just beneath the mascara, lurking just behind the eye shadow.

'Have a line,' she said, as she stared at the little tray on the coffee table. I shook my head. 'How well did you know Frank Worthington?' I asked.

'Frankie?' She smiled. 'Everybody knows Frankie.'

'Knew.'

'Why would I want to hurt little Frankie?' she said. 'Bastard owes me eight hundred dollars. You should ask around down at the Monkey's Paw, or ask your friend McGovern, if the cops ever let him go. Sure you don't want a line?'

'No, thanks,' I said. 'I had an apple on the train.'

I left. On impulse I stopped at the second landing and tried McGovern's door. It was locked. I took out another old key and cajoled my way into McGovern's apartment. The place was cluttered and dirty as hell, with record albums, books, newspapers, and news copy all over the place. It should have been clean, at least in the cop sense of the word, but I had a nagging prescience that it wasn't.

The remnants of a two-day-old Chicken McGovern were still wallowing in a blood-red sort of crusty paste in a pot on the stove. I tried some. It wasn't bad. I took a look around and was starting to leave when something caught my eye over by the stereo. McGovern's turntable was very important to him. A guy like me, who'd worked the road and made a living writing and performing music – I hated most music. Only listened to it in elevators. A guy like McGovern, who spent his time covering the seamy, late-breaking side of life, he loved music. Couldn't get enough of it. Music was his life.

He did have some taste, though. Billie Holiday was on the turntable. Through the clear plastic top I saw a pink slip lying suggestively on top of Billie. It was a bill of sale from the little flower shop around the corner on Hudson Street.

The bill came to forty-four dollars for one dozen long-stemmed pink roses.

## 4

It was a beautiful bright and cold Saturday afternoon in late February. I had pocketed the florist's receipt and locked the door on the way out and was now riding home in a cab driven by a man named Abdul bin Abdul. At least that's what it said on his hack license. He was a non-English speaker or else very shy. Either one was okay. I needed to think.

Could my large, kind, intelligent Irish drinking pal of almost a decade be involved in this bizarre business? He would make a terribly awkward murderer and an even worse bisexual, but who really knew? Somebody was working overtime to set him up and I doubted it would be Adrian. But Adrian clearly knew something and probably more than that.

I looked out of the cab. People behind windows of cozy little cafés drinking their cappuccino, spreading grapefruit marmalade on their croissants. Young couples in the streets shopping aimlessly for flavored toilet soaps.

It almost made you glad to be alive. Almost.

I took out a cigar and began the prenuptial arrangements on it. The cabbie broke the silence, pointed to the sign: 'No smoke! No smoke!' he said sullenly.

'Relax, pal,' I said, 'I wouldn't dream of it.' I put the unlighted cigar in my mouth and watched his swarthy visage checking me out in the rearview.

'So much for the Third World,' I said, as we snaked our way down Seventh Avenue toward Vandam.

I looked out the window again in silence.

It was a quiet little village. It was home to 250,000 homosexuals, and about 90,000 hard-drug abusers. And occasionally, a rather kinky little murder.

I could see the Village clearly now, but I had the chilling impression I was a long way from being out of the woods.

## 5

The Monkey's Paw was not the kind of place Ingrid Bergman might walk into some night. You wouldn't even want to see your ex-wife walk into the place.

It used to be mostly a writer's bar, a crime reporter's hangout, and I guess you could say it still is. McGovern was eighty-sixed from there years ago for peeing on the leg of a patron. It's hard to go downhill from there but the Monkey's Paw tries. Tonight I had business there.

The Weasel arrived at the Monkey's Paw always at six and always alone. He looked like a weasel. If he had a little facial tic or maybe a discernible twitch to his body you could be sure his current batch of weasel dust was the McCoy. I ran out of credit with him long ago, and fortunately, I saw him only rarely now. Like when I wanted to celebrate a death in the family.

The Weasel had a warehouse of information. About the only thing he didn't know was that his name was The Weasel.

He thought it was Max.

'Hi, Max,' I said. 'Frank Worthington working tonight?'

It was 6.05 p.m. Weasel was running a little behind his schedule.

'Don't you read the papers?' He laid the evening edition of the *Post* on the bar.

'Well! I look in on Nancy and Sluggo occasionally. Why?'

I didn't have to look too far. It was page 1. I sipped my Guinness and took a casual glance at the story: DAILY NEWS MAN HELD IN BIZARRE VILLAGE MURDER.

'Your old buddy,' said The Weasel, 'McGovern.'

'Yeah,' I said, 'I knew McGovern'd come to no good.'

Four Guinnesses later I was pumping The Weasel pretty well. I was buying him Rémys, and each time he left for his office, which was the men's room, with a client, I'd scribble down a little more information. It wasn't particularly adding up but it was a side of the case I was sure the cops didn't have. From the look of the *Post* story, I didn't even think they wanted it.

It seemed Worthington was pretty well liked and a fairly good little church worker, but he definitely had swung from both sides of the box.

And he got around pretty good too. By the time I left the Monkey's Paw, I had sort of a hazy, mental picture of four people. I knew the names of four of Worthington's current flames. At least they'd been current before last night.

I had hardly patted the cat before the phones rang. It was McGovern's girlfriend. 8.45 p.m. Cynthia was a little upset about McGovern's incarceration. I coaxed her down from the chandelier, cradled the blower, and fished a pretty nice-looking dead cigar out of the trash.

I stoked it up and listened for a while to the rhythmic thud of the lesbian dance class in the loft above me. It was run by a girl named Winnie Katz. She was making quite a name for herself among the diesel-dyke community in the Village. Might come in handy before this whole thing was over. A fellow never knew.

It was ten o'clock Saturday night, and the sidewalks of the Village were crowded with people desperately trying to have fun and some people actually having it, whatever it is. Almost none of them lived in the Village. They just periodically descended upon it whenever Brooklyn, Queens, the Bronx, New Jersey, or the plasticine Upper East Side of Manhattan became too much for them Most old-time Village residents resented them and hoped they'd get mugged. I didn't care what they got as long as it was out of my way.

Andrew had held a table for me at the Derby on MacDougal Street. The Derby is the oldest and best steak house in the Village and maybe the whole town. Andrew was busy seating customers and cursing vegetarians and young people in general for saying bad things about red meat. The trend today was toward vegetables and fish and it wasn't good for America or the Derby.

I told him to try to guess who my dinner companion would be when he came in the door. He said he'd try and I said I'd try a few shots of Jameson.

If Andrew was cursing vegetarians, I was cursing McGovern. McGovern was my main source for information on anything and he was a good one. I wouldn't call him punctual, or reliable, or even sober some of the time, but he was always a steady man in a shaky universe. I had come to think of him as sort of my American Doctor Watson, a notion he once good-naturedly described as 'stupid and self-serving.' Whatever he thought wasn't going to make too much difference to a tree, however, because he was drinking from a tin cup in the sneezer and I was going to be all alone on this one.

I looked up in time to see Andrew graciously ushering Ratso over to my table. Ratso was an old friend of mine and the editor of a wide-circulation national magazine. He was attired in a manner that was bizarre even for the Derby's rather informal dress code, but Andrew was glossing that one over apparently and ignoring the stares of the other diners. Good for him.

Ratso was wearing his usual cold-weather headgear: a coonskin cap minus the tail. He had on a black-leather motorcycle jacket and sort of off-lox-colored slacks with bright red shoes that had once belonged to a dead man. This was true of almost his entire wardrobe because he did all his shopping among the flea markets along Canal Street.

I'd often mentioned to him that the constant wearing of dead men's shoes might not be his smartest move in terms of hygiene.

He always walked away from that one by saying that before goods were sold at the flea market, they had to pass rigid tests for all these things; there was quality control, they sterilized everything, etc.

Then I would take a somewhat more spiritual approach with him, saying that I couldn't be sure but I felt that the wearing of dead men's shoes was probably not particularly good karma. Just wasn't quite best foot forward and all that. He'd always sidestep that one too, and point out some obscure Hasidic commandment that no one on earth had ever believed in, much less bothered to practice.

'Good thing nobody asked you who your tailor is,' I said. 'He's probably been dead for a hundred years.'

'Let's order,' he said.

The evening was not a total loss as it turned out. The sliced steak with the Colman's Hot English Mustard was strictly top drawer and the Jameson-Guinness combination was beginning to kick in as well.

One of the few qualities that I admire in Arabian and Turkish peoples is that they never talk serious business until the coffee has arrived. 'So, Ratso,' I said when the coffee had arrived, 'let me fill you in on the McGovern situation.' I filled him in.

'Why don't we just call it your new case?' He laughed. 'I mean, the cops think McGovern did it and we know he's innocent, right?'

'Partially,' I said. 'We believe he's innocent, yes.'

'Jesus.'

'And we know He's innocent.'

'Then who done it, Sherlock?'

'Well, not counting McGovern or the little girl who lives upstairs and sells cocaine, we have four current names to run down.' I wrote The Weasel's list of Frank's favorites down on a cocktail napkin and Ratso studied them.

'Never heard of any of them. They're all Greek to me,' he said, handing back the napkin.

'Yeah, two of them were Greek to Frank, too.' I said.

We split the list, Ratso taking the two boys and me taking the two girls, and Ratso assuring me he didn't mind 'working the homosexual side of the street if it would help McGovern.'

Ratso had good connections. He knew Spider Webb, a renowned Village tattoo artist, and he had friends who frequented such places as the Hellfire Club. I told the Rat to get on it very fast. The cops, I understood, always feel that after the first twenty-four hours the bloom begins to fade on a homicide case. After the first few days, if no big breaks develop, the case will probably only be solved by chance. The bloom on this one was fading faster than Frank Worthington's flowers. I paid the check.

## 6

Sunday morning when I woke up I did not feel like John Denver. The cat was meowing and the phones were ringing but at least the garbage trucks were silent. It was Wolf Nachman on the phone. The computer said 9.17 a.m. 'Ah,' he said, 'you're back from church already.'

'Yeah.'

'Must have been a pretty short sermon.' Humor was not particularly one of Wolf's long suits. He didn't know it though, so I had to play along.

'Yeah,' I said.

'I thought you might like to know the gun they found in McGovern's apartment is back from ballistics. It was the murder weapon.'

'What was the gun, Wolf?'

'Let's see. It says here a Beretta twenty-five caliber automatic.'

'Standard purse gun,' I said. I knew that much. I didn't know too much else about guns except I'd never owned one and never wanted to. If anybody ever croaked me, they had damn sure better remember to bring their own gun.

'Kind of looks like some broad may have Sam Cooke'd him,' I said.

'Who's that?' asked the lawyer. He wasn't really well-versed in a number of areas, including the area of Negro soul singers croaked by jealous women in hotels in America. But he knew his law. When it came to that he was as brilliant as a barracuda.

'Rather an effeminate weapon for a big boy like McGovern, wouldn't you say?'

Wolf wouldn't say. He'd seen McGovern and proceeded to tell me about it. He said he'd get back to me.

I took the pink receipt slip from the florist shop, stuffed it in an envelope, and slid it to the bottom of the cat litter tray, which I always kept in the shower except of course when I was taking a shower.

Now I was probably obstructing justice or something. At the very least I was withholding and concealing evidence directly related to a homicide case. It was kind of fun actually. And there was no other choice in the matter. If I turned the florist receipt over to Fox and told him where I'd found it, it would hang McGovern for sure.

McGovern was being kept at Central Holding behind the courthouse at 100 Centre Street. Wolf thought he would have him out on bail sometime early in the week. He could be visited only by an attorney or a clergyman and I wasn't either one of them. I didn't even want to be either one of them when I grew up.

This thing was going to take time. I took the cocktail napkin from the Derby out of a cigar box and studied the two names again; Darlene Rigby and Nina Kong.

I knew a little less about women than I knew about guns. Nobody really understood women except maybe bisexual hairdressers. They knew a lot about women but it was obvious they didn't care. In fact, women had very few friends in the world. I'd often felt that a man without a woman was like a neck without a pain.

But maybe I was being a little too harsh. I'd known many women who weren't like other women. Gunner, for instance. I wondered if she'd like to go to the Ranger game with me tonight. She was blond, British, and beautiful, and she'd never seen a hockey game. To live and die on this planet without even seeing a hockey game was something hard to imagine. People did it all the time though. They did a lot of other things too. Like stab their mother-in-law in the nose with an ice pick.

I tried not to think of McGovern down there at 100 Centre Street in a holding tank quite possibly full of hardened criminals. Gentle, good-natured McGovern, who had once combed his hair before meeting a racehorse.

I hoped he liked baloney sandwiches.

It was still a little too early to try to call Rigby or Kong. So I made some hot chocolate and sipped it for about twenty minutes while I listened to my hair grow. Then I tried information for Darlene Rigby. I knew she was a struggling young actress. Weren't they all. And I knew she lived in some big complex for the arts on Forty-third Street in the heart of Hell's Kitchen. An entire building full of young actors and dancers and the like, all struggling to make it. Well, they certainly picked the right location. In that neighborhood getting to the corner store for a pack of cigarettes was a struggle.

The Weasel had described Darlene Rigby as very talented, very beautiful, and very determined to get to the top of her profession. She might have been very talented, but if she was the one who croaked Frank Worthington, she'd taken the scene right out of a bad movie. There was something rather frightening about the campy way the whole thing was put together: the flowers, the note on the floor, the stagy table setting complete with the Bloody Marys. And the wound that itself was not very bloody, yet was emphatically evil in its perfection. A neat, rather artistic little bull's-eye that told you Frank Worthington had celebrated his very last Ash Wednesday.

If Darlene Rigby had that much determination, God help Hollywood. I picked up the phone.

'Good morning, Miss Rigby. This is Fred Barkin. I was a friend of Frank Worthington's and we're having a little informal get-together tonight at around eight o'clock at Chumley's in the Village. Do you know it? . . . Fine. Then we'll count on seeing you? . . . Fine. Just share a few drinks and a few memories for Frank . . . Yes it was . . . Terrible . . . Yes, we all do. We all do . . . It'll be the kind of evening Frank would have enjoyed. Glad you can make it . . . See you tonight. Good-bye.'

I was laying it on fairly thick, but I have found that in this business, one of the most important things is sincerity. If you can fake that, you can do just about anything.

## 7

Nina Kong might be more difficult. She was the lead singer with some new-wave country band that was in the process of signing a big recording contract. I ran her down through my friend Cleve, who was the manager of the Lone Star Café, a country-music place on Fifth Avenue and Thirteenth Street. She'd played there a few times recently, and I'd played there a few times myself back when coffee with a friend was still a dime.

'So when you gonna play here again, man?' Cleve had asked.

'Probably on a cold day in Jerusalem, pal,' I'd told him. I missed performing there like I missed having a mescal worm in my matzo-ball soup.

'Come on, man, let's work something out. You don't want people to start calling you the Legendary What's-his-name, do you? Hell, everybody can use a little exposure.'

I had forgotten how tedious Cleve could be. That was one of the things I liked about my new life-style – it hardly required my presence. If it wasn't for McGovern, I'd be taking it easy, putting the final touches on my Broadway score, getting ready to start selecting chorus girls.

'I don't want exposure, Cleve. I know people who died of exposure. How about you expose this broad's telephone number to me right now?'

I got it, got off the blower, and was in the process of removing the cat litter from the rain-room when the phones rang again.

Ratso. 10.27 a.m. 'Start talking,' I said. 'And make it fast. I'm a nudist.'

'Well, I just wanted to discuss some of the ramifications with you, Inspector Maigret.'

'That's cute, but put a sock on it, pal. What the hell do you want?' I was usually pretty grumpy but I was always pretty grumpy in the morning. I was going to make a great old person if I ever lived that long.

We coordinated the Chumley's get-together. Ratso would get his two there and I would get my two there and then we'd throw back a few toasts to ol' Frank and see what happened next. Sounded like fun. It wasn't every night you could be pretty certain you were hoisting a few with a murderer.

I hung up the phone and jumped back into the rain-room. Now there was a place I didn't mind singing.

The sun was flooding into the loft pretty impressively by now. I was feeling better after the shower. I stood at the kitchen window in my purple bathrobe and brown slippers, smoking my early morning cigar. It didn't look like February in New York. If you ignored the garbage trucks, the warehouses, the fire escapes, and the newspapers and crap blowing all over the sidewalks, it was a beautiful view. If you turned your neck at a rather extreme angle you could just see the Hudson River over to the west, but it was hard to keep your head twisted in that position for very long. The fire escapes were hard on the eyes but they were a lot easier on the neck.

I now had to make one of the hardest decisions a person living in the Village ever has to make: espresso or cappuccino. I decided upon cappuccino and walked over to the machine. I didn't have to walk too far. It took up about half of the kitchen. In the brilliant sunlight it gleamed like a small Fascist tank.

As the machine steamed and gurgled, I checked the hockey schedule on the kitchen wall. Obviously tonight was out, but Wednesday night the Rangers played their archrivals, the Islanders, at the Garden. The match-up looked brutal enough to warm the heart of any hockey fan. I considered calling Gunner, but I still had this Kong dame to take care of.

I threw a little cinnamon and a little Jameson into the cappuccino, walked over to the living-room couch, sat down, and dialed the Kong girl's number on the phone there. This was a private line. Only three or four people had this number and I wasn't even sure I remembered who they were. The rocking chair belonged to the cat.

'Good morning. Is Nina there?'

A guy answered kind of gruffly, 'Who wants to know?'

'This is Phil Bender. I'm a booking agent working for Cleve at the Lone Star.'

Nina picked up the phone.

'That was a pleasant fellow,' I said.

'Sorry about that. If this is about a booking, you're wasting your time. You can tell Cleve I won't be available for a while.'

I could see I'd have to take another tack.

'No,' I said, 'this isn't about a booking. This is about a croaking. I'm looking into Frank Worthington's murder, and if you don't want a command performance at the Sixth Precinct, I think you should cooperate with me and tell me what you know. Maybe we can keep the cops out of this.'

She didn't say anything.

I could see I'd have to take another tack. Pretty soon I wouldn't have enough left to crucify last year's calendar.

'Nina,' I said, 'this isn't Phil Bender. This is Kinky.'

'It sure is,' she said. 'I know who you are. I saw you play at the Lone Star a long time ago.'

'Yeah,' I said. 'I was probably playing there when you were jumping rope in the schoolyard. Like I said, I'm looking into this Frank Worthington thing. You've heard about Frank Worthington?'

'Y-yes,' she said. 'It's horrible.'

'Terrible,' I said. 'Look, we're having an informal little wake tonight at Chumley's in the Village. Can you make it? I'd like to talk to you.'

'Okay. What time?'

'Eight.'

'I'll be there. You know,' she said wistfully. 'I can't believe Frank's really dead. I just can't believe it.'

I took a healthy puff on my cigar. 'Pinch yourself,' I said.

# 8

The telephone was an amazing instrument for love, for business deals, and for the gathering and gleaning of information. But it had its limits. Even a quasi-legendary detective had to do a little legwork now and then. Put the violin and the cocaine syringe up on the mantel and fish the old magnifying glass out of the hope chest. I didn't much like running all over the place looking for clues but it beat jogging.

If I was one step ahead of the police, it was only because I knew McGovern was incapable of the crime and they didn't. Assuming anyone is really incapable of anything.

Maybe Wolf and I would get McGovern out and the very first thing he'd do would be to come over to my loft and croak me. Maybe the *Post* would run another headline: COUNTRY SINGER CROAKED BY DAILY NEWS MAN. Everybody could use a little exposure.

It was a beautiful afternoon to joust at windmills so I walked up Hudson in the direction of Jane Street. Cynthia, McGovern's latest girlfriend, had told me she'd probably be over at his place cleaning up a bit and straightening up his affairs. That was a good one.

I was feeling ambivalent about my visit to McGovern's the day before. I was glad I'd gone before Cynthia cleaned the place up. But what the hell was that receipt for the flowers doing there? I'd have to ask McGovern if I ever spoke to him again. I'd also like to know how many people besides the cops, the super, me, and Cynthia had keys to his apartment. Maybe he stood under the windmill and passed them out to street traffic.

Cynthia looked like a slightly weatherbeaten cheerleader. But only slightly. And that was pretty good for New York. She wanted to hug me and I let her. It didn't cost anything and I'd hugged worse in my time. I didn't like it much, though. I felt awkward, impatient about it. Hugging distraught women was just probably not one of my long suits. Of course, the distraught women never knew the difference.

'Cynthia, did McGovern call you anytime Friday evening?'

'Let me think. Yes. He called me twice. The first time he called to make sure I was coming over for dinner that night.'

'Chicken McGovern,' I said, and nodded knowingly.

'Yes.' She was starting to cry again.

'Pace yourself,' I said, 'this could be a fairly long ordeal for all of us. What was the second call about?'

'He said not to come over. That there'd been a murder in the building. 'Across the hall,' he said. Then he said, "Do you believe in ghosts?" '

## 9

I cased the whole apartment and came up with nothing but an old cowboy hat of mine from 1979. Not a particularly good year as I recalled so I tried not to. The hat was about seven sizes too small for McGovern so I really couldn't be too accusatory about the whole thing. I put it on and started to leave, telling Cynthia not to worry, the worst they could pin on him would be a second-degree murder charge and everybody knew you had to kill at least two people in New York before they even thought about putting you away.

That didn't seem to have quite the desired effect, and I wasn't going to get hugged twice on the same day, so I said we'd keep in touch and I left. She was really quite a pretty girl if you liked blondes.

I walked across the hall and took a look, but Worthington's door was locked and an NYPD 'scene of crime' seal signed by Detective Sergeant Buddy Fox was firmly in place. The cops used the seal to keep away the curious, the looters, and the ghouls. I guess you'd have to say that I fit into category one there. At least category one. For the whole weekend I'd been having intermittent yet intense struggles with Satan, who'd been urging me to break in there and have a little look in Frank Worthington's closets.

The forces of good triumphed on this occasion. I'd need professional help with the police lock anyway, and Sunday afternoon wasn't the most intellectual time selection for a breaking and entering operation. 'Maybe you should come back in the dead of the night,' the voice of Satan whispered.

'Now you're talkin' turkey,' I said.

On impulse I hoofed it up to the next landing and knocked on Adrian's door. There was a guy just leaving. At least he scurried out of there like a New York rat before I could get into the room.

Adrian looked her lovely self. She was wearing some kind of a black and red leather outfit that didn't do much for her. There wasn't really much you could do. I wished Satan could have been there to get a load of it. 'Nice,' I said, approvingly.

'Glad you like it,' she said, very possibly blushing. I couldn't really tell for sure because of the dim light in the room, the heavy makeup on her face, and my own disinclination to look too closely. It was like staring at a burned-out sun with the naked eye. It wasn't really dangerous, but it wasn't especially good for you either.

'I've been working on stained-glass art,' she said, pointing to a small, purplish pane. 'It's really time-consuming. It takes forever. I've been working on it for about six months. A friend of mine has a gallery on the Lower East Side and he's going to put it in an exhibition there.'

Every drug dealer I'd ever met was not really a drug dealer. He or she was really an artist working with stained glass, or really an author getting ready to do research for a novel about Paris in the twenties, or really a film director patiently waiting for a screenplay that accurately reflected life in Southern California. No drug dealer ever thought of himself as a drug dealer. If you asked him what he did for a living, he couldn't very well answer: 'I suck away about seventy percent of your life blood, your spirit, and your energy. Then I suck away about eighty percent of your income. Then I suck away about one hundred percent of whatever little chance you have of finding any happiness in life.'

'Nice,' I said, holding the stained glass up to what light there was.

I walked home down Fourth Street on a route that would take me through Sheridan Square and down Seventh Avenue to

Vandam. The evening was beautiful and crisp, just beginning to chill like a fine imported wine. Or a freshly croaked stiff.

It was like pulling teeth from a buzz saw but Adrian had finally agreed to leave her apartment and join us later tonight at Chumley's. That ought to round out the wake nicely, I thought.

I pulled a cigar out of my hunting vest, from one of a row of tiny pockets stitched into it to hold shotgun shells. I never hunted for anything anyway except maybe trouble.

It wasn't a bad evening and it wasn't a bad cigar either. I began entertaining thoughts of just dropping by the Sixth Precinct and shmoozing with some of the boys. Fox and Cooperman weren't especially big fans of my music. Nor were they particularly inclined to celebrate my brief but thus far successful career in the field of amateur detective work. They had no time for amateurs. When Fox and Cooperman bungled things, it was always in a polished and professional manner.

The press had been more laudatory where I had been concerned. When I had successfully wrapped up a rather grisly murder episode at the Lone Star the year before, it had made page 1 in both the *Post* and the *Daily News*. *The New York Times* must have given the order to 'Hold the back pages' when they got the story because it only made page 11. Another reason I never read *The New York Times*.

The *News* had emphasized the fact that the case had baffled the cops for months. The story had gone on to say that my efforts had 'cracked the case' and that I had provided the police with the 'stunning solution.'

The Lone Star was dead in the middle of Fox and Cooperman's bailiwick, and this kind of publicity wasn't calculated to make the three of us fast friends. The by-line, of course, had been McGovern's, but a reporter only writes what he sees.

When I got to Sheridan Square, I stopped in at Village Cigars before heading over to the cop shop. Years ago a guy wearing a cowboy hat in this area would probably have created quite a little stir. People would be yelling 'Hey, Tex' and 'Cowboy!' You never could tell if they were being derisive or just curious and exuberant, but personally, I never did like it much. If I'd been a real cowboy

I probably would have liked it even less. But then, what would a real cowboy be doing in the Village anyway? I thought they always hung out on the Upper East Side.

Of course, today cowboy hats didn't mean very much. You could drive a whole wagon train down just about any street in the Village and people would just think you were a group of happy homosexuals. Time sure changes the river.

I took a left on Tenth Street and walked the two blocks west to the Sixth Precinct station house. A large green globe glimmered on either side of the steps, showing the pedestrians where to enter and the Sunday pigeons where to sit. A sign was posted on one of the glass doors: ALL VISITORS MUST STOP AT FRONT DESK. No problem there.

A Sergeant Bello was at the muster desk. I asked for Fox or Cooperman. I don't know if you could say my luck was in but both of them were. Bello picked up a phone and a moment later Fox came into the doorway behind the muster desk. He was grinning unpleasantly. 'Hi, cowboy!' he said. Some things never change.

He gave me what he evidently thought was a coy little wink and motioned Bello to open the drawbridge. I angled under the raised top of the muster desk and followed Fox down a hallway past the detention cages. He opened a pebbled-glass door that said SQUAD ROOM in black letters. There were metal filing cabinets lining three of the walls and there were four desks in the room. Detective Mort Cooperman sat behind one of them, leaning back in a wooden chair, one leg looped over a corner of the desk. He was smoking and smirking at the same time.

'Your boy's not here,' he said.

'Yeah,' I said, 'we knew that.'

'We? We?' he said. 'What's the matter, you got a mouse in your pocket?'

Fox sat down behind another desk. I remained standing, partly so I could be able to make a quick getaway, but mainly because nobody had asked me to sit down.

'My lawyer and I know where our boy is, but we think our son is innocent,' I said, trying to leaven the situation a bit. A guy going through a filing cabinet in the corner chuckled, but Fox and Cooperman weren't having any.

'Did you find out who the gun belonged to?'

'Yeah,' said Fox. 'The gun was registered to Worthington. But the apartment it was found in was registered to your . . . uh . . . McGovern.'

'Could be a clue, don't you think?' said Cooperman, as he crushed a Gauloise into the ashtray. I wasn't going to comment on his off brand of cigarettes. He probably thought he was a special agent for the French Secret Service. 'Look,' he said, 'McGovern will be out on bail soon, probably with a second-degree murder rap; then in a few weeks time, he'll go before the grand jury. He hasn't been talking much, you know.'

'What's to say?' said Fox. 'It's fairly dead to rights.'

'Maybe there's an angle that hasn't really been pursued,' I said.

'What would that be,' asked Cooperman. 'That Worthington shot McGovern?'

'No. It would be that Worthington was a rather promiscuous bisexual with some pretty interesting bedfellows.'

'Well, I don't know, guy,' said Fox.

'Half the friggin' Village is bi,' said Cooperman. 'And the other half is pure fruit.'

'Present company excluded of course,' I said with a friendly smile.

'Yeah,' said Cooperman, as he got up and walked over to the hat rack to get his brim.

'Nice rack,' I said. 'I thought those things went out with the buggy whip.'

'Get out,' said Fox.

'Then you're not going to pursue the angle?'

'Get out,' said Fox again, 'and try using your head for something more than a hat rack.'

I left, sailing back out under the drawbridge, giving a smart left-handed salute to Sergeant Bello, and stepping out into the street. The pigeons were still nestling on the two green globes. If the wheels of justice were turning, the pigeons didn't know it.

## 10

Even a wake where you don't know the stiff can be a fairly strenuous thing. Not that it was going to be that kind of wake. I wasn't even sure that any of the wakers really cared. Well, obviously one of them had.

Nonetheless, by the time I got back to the loft on Vandam I was feeling like the Invisible Man on a bad day, except I knew I couldn't be him because I was still wearing the cowboy hat when I walked in. It was almost as if I hadn't got out of bed, and the whole afternoon had been spent in a slow-walking dream.

I hadn't learned much from Cynthia Floyd except that her last name was Floyd.

With Fox and Cooperman it was like I'd never spoken to them at all. Just stopped at the visitor's desk to admire the black, hairy caterpillar that was resting on Bello's upper lip. They listened to me about as seriously as the Trojans had listened when Cassandra had told them, 'Don't bring that wooden horse into the city.'

If I'd told them about the bill of sale from the florist shop that was now comfortably residing in my cat-litter tray, they probably would have hanged me and McGovern with the same rope. And of course they would have loved to hear about McGovern's ghost. That story probably would have landed the two of us a free suite on the fifth floor of Bellevue.

I decided to take a little power nap, and when I woke up it was dark outside and pushing seven o'clock. I made a double espresso and lighted a cigar. Then I put on some suitable somber clothing, including a tie that said HELLO. HANDSOME but could only be read when you looked at it in a mirror.

I was about as ready as I was ever going to be to see and be seen. I took the freight elevator down.

If you headed up Hudson and then took a right at Barrow and continued until you came to Bedford, you would be at Chumley's, only you still wouldn't be at Chumley's. The place had been a speakeasy during Prohibition and there had never been so much as a sign, a number, or even a light to mark its location on the street. It remains that way today. Most people just walk right by the place, and if I'd known where this whole thing was going to lead, I'd probably have walked on by myself.

As it was, I pushed open the wooden gate and walked into a half-dark courtyard with little else but the moonlight shining on the flagstones. The place is supposed to have been one of F. Scott Fitzgerald's favorite haunts in the Village before he went west and eventually died, a broken man, in Hollywood.

I always made a point of drinking a Jameson with F. Scott whenever I came into Chumley's. Of course, you couldn't tell that Chumley's was even there until you left the quiet courtyard and pulled open another door. Then it always hit you as if you were suddenly entering an older, better world. People at the bar were laughing. A fireplace was burning brightly. Tonight Billie Holiday was on the jukebox. She really got around.

I walked over to the bar, ordered and downed a fast Jameson. Over in a far corner of the room I could see Ratso's glass raised in a toast to ol' Frank. At the table with him were two men whose identities I didn't know but could pretty well guess, and a blond thing I took to be Darlene Rigby.

They looked as if they were getting along all right so I hung out at the bar a little longer and had another Jameson with F. Scott. He was in kind of a grim mood. Probably been fighting with the wife again. You never knew with old F.

It was a good thing I had stayed awhile at the bar because Nina Kong was just walking in and she appeared hesitant enough to bolt at the drop of a G chord. Nina was dressed in a dark, velvet, spiffily tailored suit, and some women do look good in black. She looked like a sinister, Oriental doll.

She was sinister all right but she wasn't bad. Far from it. And she was doing a few things with her upper lip that I hadn't seen before this side of the Ho Chi Minh Trail.

I walked over to her and took her by the arm. 'The others are waiting,' I said. 'Sorry I had to be so brusque on the phone this morning.'

'And I'm sorry if I was rude,' she said. 'I really don't have the personality of a one-thousand-year-old egg, you know.' Her voice and manner were those of a modern American girl, but her eyes were flickering with Eastern mischief. They were terrific. And then there was the upper lip.

She could smile, sulk, beckon, or point in either direction with it. She could probably kill you with it.

'Do you know any of these people?' I asked as we neared the Ratso party.

'I've never seen any of them before,' she whispered close to my ear.

'Good,' I whispered back. She smiled and her smile looked good, too. Good enough to melt somebody's Dreamsicle.

Ratso and the two guys stood up and made room for us around the table as I introduced Nina to the group and Ratso introduced me as 'The Kinkster.' 'Kinky was a dear friend of Frank's,' Ratso said, as he avoided my eyes. God knows what he'd been telling these people. Flying by bisexual radar could be dangerous even for an experienced pilot.

Darlene Rigby introduced herself. She was an attractive type but she was still a type. She was an actress and I suppose the question would always be 'Is that really her or is she only acting?' That is, if anybody gave a damn about it besides her acting coach who was probably just trying to bed her down himself. I hadn't cared much for actresses since Jean Harlow had died.

The two guys and Ratso stood up, sat down, ordered more drinks, and continued to look like themselves. If I'd been expecting anybody to show any glint of recognition, any veiled hostility, or any telltale evasiveness, I'd have been very disappointed. It didn't look as if anybody knew anybody. Everybody was in their own little innocent world. Even Ratso seemed to be ignoring me.

One of the guys was named Pete Myers, a fairly dapper Englishman as they go, with a little blue scarf-tie around his neck. He looked like the type who would have gotten there on a bicycle, and as it turned out he had. I couldn't really hold that against him but every quirk adds up.

The other guy, who completed the sandwich around Darlene Rigby, was a handsome devil named Barry Campbell, who looked like he'd either just come in from the Islands or else had been working the sunlamp overtime. Either way he looked a shade too healthy and nobody likes that. Particularly in New York.

Both of the guys looked pretty gay for a wake. I hadn't yet been able to glean what they did. I mean, I knew some of the things they did, but what they actually did I didn't know.

I didn't get to find out right then for two reasons. One: As I started to lean forward, Ratso gave me a little sign with his hand that I took to mean things were cool, he had everybody lamped perfectly, and two: Adrian made her slinking little entrance, fashionably late in keeping with her profession as a stained-glass artist. It appeared she knew everybody but me, Ratso, and Darlene. I ordered more drinks.

'How long have you known Adrian?' I asked Nina.

'We go way back,' Adrian said before Nina could separate her lips. Adrian was chatting away like a large, amoral chipmunk, but it was having the effect of keeping the ball rolling so I contented myself with a little Nina Kong eye contact.

We'd been sitting there a good fifteen minutes and no one had even mentioned Frank yet. I was waiting to see who'd be first and hoping that nobody would ask me anything. I might step on something and it probably wasn't going to be third base.

'He was a beautiful man,' said Nina at last.

'A stunningly beautiful man,' said Peter Myers.

'Perhaps too beautiful for his own good,' said Barry Campbell.

'How did you know Frank, Kinky?' It was Darlene. Her voice would've carried to the balcony if there'd been one. She had a sort of little happy-sad, expectant smile on her face. I wanted to knock it off with a right cross.

'We go way back, too,' I said, a trifle too sullenly.

If you think picking out a murderer from a group of people sitting around a table is easy, you should try it sometime. Nobody was giving anything away. And whoever offed Frank Worthington was methodical, painstakingly careful, and had a nice eye for detail. He or she belonged to the cream of the criminal class. We were dealing with a murderer who had mastered whatever it means to be normal but was really anything but. Thinking about it didn't really get me anything but a few goose pimples. I ordered another round of drinks.

Ratso wanted a screwdriver. Pete predictably wanted a Pimm's Cup Number something or other. Adrian had a Perrier. Darlene ordered some kind of white-wine drink that actresses drink. It was a cumbersome and time-consuming order, and she had to explain it several times to the waiter, much to the irritation of serious drinkers like me and Barry Campbell.

When the waiter finally looked at me, I went with a 'Bloody Wetback,' a drink an old girlfriend and I had pioneered out on the West Coast. It was a double shot of José Cuervo tequila, a glass of tomato juice, and a lemon. Of course, the whole evening was beginning to look like a lemon.

That was until Barry Campbell laughed and ordered a big pitcher of Bloody Marys. He wasn't looking at the waiter. He was looking straight at Nina Kong, and quite distinctly, I watched him wink at her.

Now the fact that a pitcher of Bloody Marys was found at the scene of the crime was privileged information that the police had withheld from the press. It is routine procedure in a homicide case for them to keep a few things like this up their sleeves. That way, when fourteen sick chickens confessed to killing Frank Worthington, they might all presumably know about the method of death and the flowers, but only the guilty one would know that Frank Worthington had been drinking a pitcher of Bloody Marys with his killer.

This either cleared Campbell completely, I figured, or else he was very stupid or else he was very smart. Take your pick.

Nine Kong said she was ready to leave. She looked as white as she was ever going to. She told us she had a rehearsal for a video they were doing tomorrow.

'I'll help you get a cab,' I said.

'That won't be necessary.'

I did anyway, and when we got outside I saw why it wouldn't be necessary. A limo and driver were waiting for her at the curb.

'Can I take you somewhere?' she asked.

'No,' I said. 'What I'd really like is a home video of your upper lip.'

She laughed. About half innocently and half knowingly, I thought. She was terrific but I wondered what else she was.

We sat in back for a while swapping phone numbers and hobbies. She took out an enameled Oriental-style snuffbox full of Peruvian-style snuff. We both took a pinch or two.

'This couldn't be Adrian's stuff, could it?' I asked. I knew it wasn't. Adrian's stuff always looked like it'd been stepped on by the Budweiser Clydesdales.

'No, it's from the record company. So's the limo.'

'I wish you all the best,' I said. I knew as well as anybody what a small step it was from the limo to the gutter. I also knew that we'd all get a limo again when we were dead so I wasn't worried. I never took limos, I never took subways, and I never took private French lessons advertised in the Village.

We nipped a few more little pinches of snuff. 'Are you sure you've never seen Barry Campbell before?' I asked.

'Positive. Did you really ever know Frank Worthington?'

'Not until I saw him on the floor,' I answered.

I kissed her and we said good night. I'd see her again soon. We had a date for a hockey game on Wednesday night. She'd never seen a hockey game.

By the time I got back inside, things were breaking up. No one could understand why anybody would want to kill Frank. Like all dead people, Frank had been a 'warm and human' guy. Like all dead people, he wasn't one now.

We all shook hands and said we'd get together. Ratso said he'd call me in the morning. He was pretty bombed and I was just about walking on my knuckles.

I told the waiter to drop the hatchet, I paid the bill, and I left. The ice had almost melted in the pitcher of Bloody Marys. Sort of had a familiar look to it, like a face in a dream.

## 11

I was halfway through my first Monday morning espresso and just thinking about breaking out my first cigar of the day when the phones rang. It was Ratso. 9.47 a.m.

'I'm coming over, Sherlock. Tell your landlady . . . what's-her-name . . . to get the kippers ready.'

'Mrs Hudson, like the street. I hope you've got the goods on those guys.'

'Pete and Barry and I are like old friends.'

'Yeah, well, you better watch yourself, Rat. Sometimes old friends will stab you in the back.'

About fifteen minutes later, as I was just embarking on a second espresso, I heard Ratso screaming from the street like a young castrato.

There are no buzzers or names of occupants on the door at 199B Vandam. From the street the whole place looks like an empty warehouse, which it undoubtedly was before somebody got clever and converted the building to loft space.

I am probably less interested than you are in the history of New York real estate. People tell me it is stupid to rent if you can own the property. But I figure it this way. We are living in a time and place threatened by nuclear war, social upheaval, and biblical curses. Kind of keeps you on your toes. I always think. But for a person to actually bother to own property in a place like New York seems to me to be a rather temporal and ephemeral statement to make. Personally, I'd have more confidence in a small boy holding a butterfly's wing.

Of course it would depend upon the deal.

Ratso was yelling from the street again. Not having buzzers and intercoms at the front door had at first seemed a nuisance, but now I preferred their absence. It made it a little harder on visitors, including cops with search warrants. And there were no surprises. I didn't like surprises.

Anyway, I'd solved the problem of letting people into the building long ago when I bought a little Negro puppet on Canal Street and removed its head. The head was about the size of a small grapefruit and the eyes opened and closed. I wedged the key to the front door in its mouth. I'd attached a brightly colored home-made parachute to the head, and making some allowances for wind currents and fire-escape entanglement, I threw the whole thing down to Ratso. Bull's-eye. I was really getting good.

Five minutes later the espresso machine was steaming and humming and Ratso and I were sitting at the kitchen table.

'Monday's the day Mrs. Hudson goes to her video course at the New School,' I explained. 'Anything I can do for you while we wait for the espresso?'

'You could stop blowing that cigar smoke in my face.'

'No problem.' I got the espresso. 'All right,' I said. 'Spit it.'

Ratso had done his homework pretty well, and he filled me in on these two characters with more information than I had ever cared to know. My chief interest was in Barry Campbell, but I wasn't letting Pete Myers off the hook either.

Campbell was a dancer who worked mainly at a place called the Blue Canary. He was also a male model. Big surprise. I was sure he went way back with Frank Worthington. And I do mean back.

Campbell was a pretty boy, but I had a feeling that his face would be popping up in something pretty ugly pretty soon. Have to keep an eye on him.

Pete Myers was a bird of a different feather. His plumage wasn't quite that spectacular. He lived on Barrow Street and made meat pies, British pastries and something he called the 'British Knish,' in his own oven. He sold them to various restaurants around town that were owned and frequented by his countrymen. Myers was making it, but barely. He saw the British Knish, which he'd invented, as his main chance to trade his bicycle for a Bentley. He was lobbing his knish right at the American fast-food market.

It looked like a long shot but once you could've said the same about the french fry.

Ratso bent my ear for the better part of an hour, gave me the two phone numbers and addresses, asked about McGovern, pledged to stay on the case, and left.

I was sorry he'd mentioned McGovern because I knew less

about McGovern's situation than I did about the chances for the British Knish. One thing was for sure – when McGovern got sprung I was going to have a good long talk with him. And if he wanted to tell me a ghost story, I was ready to listen.

The next two days crawled by like a centipede with a bad case of the gout. I read the papers, answered the phones, fed the cat four times, and smoked sixteen cigars. That was a fairly large number even for me, but I only smoked them about halfway down before throwing them away for the first time. I'd always let them age a little while and then select the finest of the lot for resurrection when circumstances demanded.

Wolf Nachman had left a message on my answering machine Tuesday afternoon while I was in Chinatown. I told the cat before I left that she was in charge of everything while I was gone, but apparently she hadn't bothered to take the call from Nachman. Cats, as a rule don't like lawyers. They have great insight into human character.

The thrust of Wolf's message was not to give up. He'd have McGovern out very soon now. There'd been a few complications but it was all right now. He'd call as soon as McGovern was sprung.

By Wednesday afternoon I'd heard nothing more from Wolf, so I called him at his office. 'If we're paying you by the hour,' I said, 'I'll just be a minute.'

'Don't worry; we'll work something out,' he said. I wasn't too worried about working something out. I was just concerned with working one large innocent Irishman out of the sneezer. That didn't seem like too much to ask. But Wolf was supposed to be the best, so there was nothing for it but to wait and not let McGovern's sad state of affairs steal the puck from my enjoyment tonight at the hockey game with Nina Kong.

The New York Rangers had not won a Stanley Cup Championship since 1940, which as fate would have it was before my time. It didn't really look like they'd be wrapping one up this year either. The point of the whole thing as I saw it was to immerse yourself in the Madison Square Garden atmosphere: the ice, the fights, the crowd of hockey fanatics. And if that didn't work, there was always the game. It was a good way to leave your troubles behind, and this Wednesday evening I seemed to be having my share.

Things had been going nowhere fast. The cat was out of cat food and the litter tray wasn't looking too good either. It had never looked good but it had looked better. As for me, I was fresh out of charm. I hadn't been sleeping real well, and I hadn't shaved in a few days and was beginning to bear a very slight familial resemblance to Sirhan Sirhan. What was worse, I was beginning to understand his mind. Perfect hockey fan mentality.

I knew that even Sherlock himself used to get pretty gnarly when he was between cases, but here I was right in the middle of one and I was about as frustrated and helpless as Grogan's goat. Too many possible motives, none of which made any real sense. Fox and Cooperman were playing their cards so close to the vest you'd think they were riverboat gamblers.

Well, I knew two things for sure: one, that the lesbian dance class had just started again in the loft upstairs, and two, that McGovern had not croaked Frank Worthington. I also knew if I didn't get moving soon I'd be late meeting Nina at the hockey game. She'd be sitting in her limo snorting cocaine and wondering what to do. Poor child.

I'd left the cat in charge and my hand was twisting the doorknob to the right when the phones rang. 7.05 p.m. Game time was 7.30 p.m. and it wasn't Wolf Nachman. It was Darlene Rigby making inquiries into my health in a rather breathy voice that didn't really sound as if she cared whether I lived or died.

'Listen, Darlene, I'm on the run,' I said. 'Can you nut-shell this?'

'Yeah,' she said, 'I'll nut-shell it. It's something I remembered and it's pretty strange. It's about Frank Worthington.'

'Can you get to the meat of it? I'm running later than whoever that *Alice in Wonderland* character was who was running late.'

'I remembered something. I saw them together once. And there was something strange.'

'Look, Darlene. Will this keep till the morning?'

'Sure. I suppose, but . . .'

'Okay. I'll be at your place at ten o'clock tomorrow morning for croissants or whatever you actresses like to eat. What's the apartment number?'

'It's Forty-three-L.'

'See you in the morning. Bye.'

I hung up and left, grabbing my hat, my coat, and a cigar for the road.

As it turned out, Darlene's little secret wasn't going to keep till the morning. But how in the hell was I supposed to know?

## 12

The hockey game was not particularly one for the books but at least it was a hockey game. It wasn't a disco or a seminar on natural childbirth. Nina seemed pleasantly hypnotized by the game and the crowd. We had a few huge cups of beer, which always tasted soapy at the Garden but after a while you didn't care, and we each had foot-long hot dogs that were still barking half an hour after we'd eaten them. At the end of the first period, Nina joined the throng to the ladies' room and I went out into the foyer to make a phone call.

I had to wait while some guy from New Jersey yapped for a while to his girlfriend but that's what love is all about. The whole thing cost me only about eight minutes out of my life so I guess it was a small price to pay. Seemed fairly interminable at the time.

My call was to Cynthia Floyd, who I knew had been camping out at McGovern's place on Jane Street waiting to hear any news at all. She and McGovern had not been an item for all that long but seemed to get on well together. I could still see her little blond puppy face when I'd told her McGovern could get a second-degree murder rap. I felt sorry for her. And she was a damned sight better than McGovern's last broad, who'd been a professional Third World feminist for the United Nations.

'How are you, Cynthia?' She sounded fuzzy. Possibly she'd been getting into the wholesale whiskey warehouse that McGovern was pleased to call his liquor cabinet.

She wanted to know everything so I gave her the lot. It wasn't much. I told her very briefly about the wake at Chumley's. I told her about Nachman's most recent conversation with me. I told her Ratso and I'd be following up on Pete Myers and Barry Campbell. I told her that the struggling young actress. Darlene Rigby, might have something she wanted to get off her chest. Sounded too melodramatic to be anything but I'd probably see her in the morning.

'Cynthia? Are you there?' Maybe I'd put her on the nod.

'Yes. I'm here. What about the other girl?'

'Oh, you mean Nina Kong. She's here with me tonight. I'm getting in tight with her here at the hockey game. I'll definitely be pumping her tonight – for information only of course.'

'Oh, God. What am I going to do?'

'Look, we're going to get him out. We're going to find out who really did it. Don't worry and don't start hitting the singles-bar circuit yet. He'll be out of there any minute.'

I wish I could have believed what I was telling her, but there are times when almost anything is better than the truth. Of course I didn't even know the truth. And if somebody did know it, he was sure keeping it under his hairpiece. Maybe an old Tibetan monk, or Jesus, or the man in the moon, or the President knew the truth, but none of them was at the hockey game and I was.

The call to Cynthia had taken longer than I'd intended and had been interrupted periodically by roars, chants, and rumbles from the crowd, including several 'oohs' and 'aahs' indicating narrowly missed goals. By the time I got back to Nina, the Islanders had come back with two goals and the score was now tied 3–3. The fans were in a mood to waste any ten-year-old child carrying an Islander pennant.

It didn't really make you proud to be an American, but it did keep you awake.

In the third period the Islanders scored two more goals, but the crowd got its chance to put in its two cents when an Islander was practically knocked unconscious and had to be taken from the ice on a stretcher. They cheered lustily. They jeered. 'You better be dead!' somebody shouted.

'These people are animals,' Nina said.

'Let me help you out of the limo, baby,' I said.

We left soon afterward, slightly ahead of the exodus of angry Ranger fans from the Garden. As it turned out, I helped her into the limo and got in after her.

As we rode down to the Village we took a few more pinches and I gave her upper lip a little workout but it was nothing that D. H. Lawrence would want to write home about. I wondered what Barry Campbell was doing tonight at the Blue Canary. It was probably something Lawrence of Arabia would want to write home about.

It used to be that it took all kinds. Now it didn't even take two kinds.

## 13

Nina had the limo driver drop me at the Monkey's Paw on Bedford Street, and she continued on to wherever today's video children play when they deign to part company with their television sets and go out at night. Usually they go to places that have real television sets. I rarely watched television, I didn't dance to speak of, and I disliked most young people and green plants a good bit more than I feared the nuclear war that might destroy them. So I didn't hit the nightclub circuit much.

Neither did The Weasel. He was too busy popping in and out of the men's room, and tonight was no exception. When he finally saw me, he walked over with a worried look on his face. If you've never seen a worried Weasel, you don't ever want to. He was worried that the Worthington murder case would heat up and some of the suspects I was checking out might get wise to who put me on to them. Like the President, he felt that his job required a fairly high degree of visibility, and the idea frightened him not a little. I tried to calm him a bit. Just a bit.

'Relax, pal. Just keep your eyes open. In your line of work, you can't really call in the police, you know.'

He went back to the men's room and I wandered over to the bar. I could hardly walk into the Monkey's Paw anymore without thinking of The Bakerman. I never realized that Tom Baker had been my best friend until after he was dead. Usually works that way.

When The Bakerman's eyes twinkled, you could see the green hills of Ireland where he'd come from but had never been. I motioned to Tommy the bartender for a drink.

Tommy had been working the night a little over three years ago when Baker died. Tommy'd leaned across the crowded bar, looking even more Buddha-like than usual, and asked: 'Is it true about The Bakerman? He's gone South?'

'Yeah,' I said.

Tom Baker had been an actor, but he'd been a lot of other things too. He'd been a great one in life. But life wasn't the movies. They didn't reissue life. There weren't any reruns.

Now, as I glanced around the bar, everybody looked like gray people in a gray casino. 'Do you know The Bakerman?' I said to no one in particular. 'He lives in Drury Lane.'

I went over to the pay phone and called my friend Rambam at the Brooklyn offices of Pallorium, his security firm. Rambam was a private investigator, although I'd never really seen his license. He had spent two years in federal Never-Never land where he had picked up several handy trades and made some pretty good connections. He claimed he was still wanted in every state that begins with an *I*. He was wanted by me tonight because I wanted to get past the lock on Frank Worthington's apartment and I was running out of time.

We arranged to meet at 2.00 a.m. at the Corner Bistro, which was only a few blocks from McGovern's place and was open till 4.00 a.m. The Bistro served something called the Bistro Burger that was bigger than your head. I'd always made it a practice never to eat anything bigger than my head but I was hungry and edgy and Rambam usually ran on Brooklyn Standard Time so I ordered a Bistro Burger and told the guy to drag it through the garden.

The guy was still working on it when Rambam walked in, which gives you an idea of how fast the service at the Corner Bistro is. Rambam watched the Bistro Burger sizzling on the open grill, thought it looked pretty good, and so he ordered one too. We had a few beers. I was in no hurry. Two o'clock in the morning was almost rush-hour traffic in this area with people coming home from the bars. Three or even four o'clock would be about the right time for this particular caper, I thought.

I gave Adrian a call. Stained-glass artists, I knew, worked very late and didn't mind calls at strange hours. I told her I might be by with a friend within an hour or so. She said fine. I didn't want to bother Cynthia and I didn't want Cynthia to bother me. Adrian's place on the third floor would be a handy escape hatch if anybody showed up while Rambam and I were fooling around in front of Frank Worthington's door. I sincerely hoped Rambam was as good as he thought he was because I did not look forward to seeing Adrian at 3.30 in the morning.

'You ready, pal?' I asked.

'Yeah,' he said. 'Let me get my bowling ball out of the trunk.'

He walked up the street about a block, opened the trunk of a black Jaguar, and came walking back jauntily with a green army knapsack, about the size of a small accordion, carelessly slung around his left shoulder. 'All right,' he said. 'It's party time.'

We walked past the shadow of the windmill and right up the steps to 42 Jane, encountering no one. The building seemed pretty quiet. It was a little after 3.00 a.m.

On the stairwell of the first landing, he handed me a woolen cap, a pair of ordinary garden gloves, and a flashlight about the size of a cigarette lighter. It could be held in the hand or the mouth and was called a bite-light. The plastic over the little bulb was painted red and gave off a soft glow. Rambam stuck an earplug into his left ear. It was attached to a police scanner that he slipped around his belt and on which he monitored all communications between the local precinct and radio patrols in the area.

When we reached Worthington's door, the first thing I noticed was that the 'scene of crime' seal had been broken. Rambam was already chuckling and reaching into his knapsack. He came out with a small putty knife. 'This one's for *The Guinness Book of World Records*,' he said.

He wedged the knife tightly between the door and the door-jamb, worked it in a little farther, and then gave it a little shove with the heel of his hand. It had taken about twelve seconds if anyone was counting. I'd been too busy counting my worry beads. But he'd opened that door faster than a mob informer could go down Mulberry Street on a skateboard.

We stood inside, closed the door, and turned on the bite-lights. Rambam took an elaborate sort of mideastern bow and I patted him on the back. 'Cops broke the seal themselves,' he said. 'They're probably through in here but they could come back. Cops are sneaky.'

Every surface in the room was coated with a thick layer of dust and fingerprint powder in about equal proportions. 'If this stuff makes me sneeze, don't forget to say "God bless you," ' Rambam whispered.

'Yeah, the Irishman's tip,' I said. 'Just don't sneeze.'

'Whatever you say,' he said and started walking across the room. Everything looked about the same except that Frank Worthington wasn't at home.

I walked over to the closet, turned the knob, and pulled the closet door open a little. I couldn't see a damn thing. I opened the door all the way and we brought the two lights closer and played them around the closet.

What had apparently once been men and women's clothing had been slashed to mere ribbons and lay all over the bottom of the closet. It looked like the floor of Macy's gift-wrapping department at closing time. Only it reeked of evil.

I bent down to examine a few remnants on the floor, and something rolled off the top shelf of the closet. It was round and flesh colored and it had hair growing out of the top of it. It bounced once with a loud thud and rolled to a sullen, sickening stop in the semidarkness between us.

'Jesus Christ,' I said.

'Not quite my idea of getting a little head,' said Rambam.

The head stared up at us out of the gloom. It didn't say anything. It didn't really have to.

'Notice the moss on the dummy,' I said.

'So. What of it?' said Rambam.

'Short-hair wig,' I said. 'Almost identical to Worthington's own hair. Why would he need that?'

'How should I know?' said Rambam. 'Why does the pope shit in the woods?'

I stared down at the object on the floor and it glared balefully, eyelessly, back at me like a sentient, grotesque grapefruit.

'Precisely,' I said.

Finding the head in Worthington's apartment was not only a fairly hairraising experience, it also raised a few rather disturbing questions.

One was what the hell it was doing here.

Another was what the hell we were doing there.

## 14

I got to bed at around 5.30 a.m. I got up at 8.30 a.m. Three hours sleep. Napoleon was supposed to have got by on only two or three hours sleep every night. Maybe that was why he was so short. I didn't know and I didn't really care. I made some coffee, drank a few cups, fed the cat, and headed up the West Side to Hell's Kitchen.

You could tell Hell's Kitchen when you got there because there was a junkie hiding behind every garbage can. Sullen-looking kids from every country in the United Nations were milling restlessly about on the street corners even at this early hour of the morning. They looked like they wanted to steal somebody's cappuccino.

I found Darlene Rigby's building. I walked through the lobby, pushed the button, and waited for one of the elevators. There were eight of them in the building but they all seemed to be in perpetual motion. I was running a little late but I certainly wasn't going to leg it up forty-three floors. Sooner or later one of these elevators was going to take it into its head to come down to the lobby.

While I waited I wondered. I thought about what Darlene had said on the phone the night before. 'I remembered something,' she'd said. So far, so good. 'I saw them together once.' Whom had she seen together once? Obviously, Frank and one of our little friends. I already knew that. 'And there was something strange,' she'd said. What could be strange? In New York what could be strange?

I didn't have to wait too long to find out. The elevator doors opened and soon I was hurtling forty-three floors' worth into the heavens above New York City.

When I got out of the elevator, I took a left and followed the arrows to 43L. It was a long and fairly plushly appointed hallway and Darlene Rigby's apartment was at the extreme end of it. When I finally arrived at her door, I raised my hand to knock but that was as far as I got.

The door was already open an inch or two. I pushed it the rest of the way. It was quiet. Too quiet.

It was a pretty big place. I walked through the living room, took a casual turn through the kitchen, and backtracked again to the bedroom before I saw her.

It was a scene all right, but not the kind a Broadway audience would like to see. Darlene Rigby may have been a struggling young actress, but this time she seemed to have put up the struggle of her life.

The whole room looked as if someone had been changing the scenery on the stage set and had stopped to take a lunch break. Everything was everywhere.

She was sprawled on the bed wearing nothing but a torn night-gown and a number of ugly bruises and contusions. Her face was as white as Philadelphia cream cheese. It was starting to look a little bloated. Both her neck and one of her legs were twisted at what seemed to be quite unnatural angles.

I didn't know when the final curtain had fallen on Darlene Rigby, but she had probably been dead for quite a while. I touched her hand and it was colder than last year's reviews.

As I headed for the telephone on the night table, I stumbled on an unopened bottle of champagne on the floor. There was a little white card attached to the bottle and it had a message typed on it; 'break a leg, baby,' it said.

## 15

With the possible exception of God's, I didn't really know whose jurisdiction this crime came under. But since I already had a rapport with Fox and Cooperman, I thought I'd give them the first fling at it.

I dialed information and asked for the number of the Sixth Precinct in the Village. Darlene Rigby's number would be charged for the information call but I didn't think she'd mind.

I dialed the number. 'Sixth Precinct,' a voice answered.

'Detective Sergeant Fox, please,' I said. The call was then put through to the detectives' squad room. A familiar voice began grating in my ear.

'Special Crimes Task Force. Sergeant Fox speaking,' it said.

I spoke to the voice for a little while and the voice spoke to me. Since Fox and Cooperman were a part of the Special Crimes Task Force, their jurisdiction was the whole city. So I'd called the correct number, though the results might still prove to be a bit sticky.

'It definitely looks like foul play?' asked Fox.

'I'm afraid Ronnie Milsap could see this one,' I said. He was a blind country singer.

'Who the hell's Ronnie Milsap?' Fox screamed at me.

'He's a blind country singer,' I said. I lighted a cigar and waited.

'Listen, guy,' he said, 'we're on our way. But you are not to touch anything, you are not to leave the stiff, and you are not to smoke your goddamn cigar around the stiff.'

'Roger,' I said, but Fox apparently had already hung up the phone. My cigar and I walked into the living room together. I sat down in one of those comfortable, fan-backed bamboo chairs, put my feet up on the coffee table, and puffed away on the cigar.

The cigar wasn't bad, but I didn't know how much longer it would be able to keep the world at bay.

It took maybe sixteen minutes before the world came barging into Darlene Rigby's apartment on the forty-third floor. It came in the form of a cavalry charge led by Fox and Cooperman, followed by a locust swarm of scientists who bore the resigned expressions of another day at the office. The cheerful, rotund assistant medical examiner brought up the rear.

I wondered why assistant medical examiners were nearly always rotund. Maybe it was the way of their people.

Everybody charged right by me into the bedroom, but Fox came back out after a few minutes to say hello. To look at his face you'd think there was a piece of meat lodged in his throat.

'Okay, pal,' he said, 'I don't care who you are. Do you understand me? I don't care if your goddamn daddy invented highway reflectors. I want to know what the hell you think you're doing here calling us from this stiff's apartment?'

He sounded fairly serious.

'She called last night wanting to talk to me. It was something to do with Frank Worthington, but I was on my way out to the Garden to see the Ranger game and I was running late. So we agreed to meet here this morning at ten o'clock for breakfast.'

'So what the hell happened?' asked Fox. There was now a rather disturbing calmness about him.

'I don't really know,' I said. 'I guess somebody burned the bacon.'

I was trying to think, myself, of who might have offed Darlene Rigby and why, and what Frank Worthington's murder might have had to do with this one. I was trying to think about a lot of things but it became apparent that this wasn't the time or place for much logical deduction on my part. The old gray cells would just have to wait. Before I could use my brain, first I was going to have to save my neck.

Cooperman came into the room and stood stage right of the chair in which I was sitting. I had taken my feet off the coffee table just out of etiquette. The cigar was smoldering in a nearby ashtray.

Cooperman didn't look very friendly this morning either. 'Why don't we just run Mr Broadway in and get it over with?' he asked Fox in a voice as thick as grime on the window of a subway train.

I was starting to feel a long way from COUNTRY SINGER PLUCKS VICTIM FROM MUGGER. How soon they forget.

Cooperman's question, it appeared, was somewhat rhetorical. At least for the time being. Fox preferred to grill me right then and there. I told them the names of the three people, obviously excluding Darlene Rigby, who I felt might know something about the Worthington case. This time, I noticed, they at least took the time to write the names down, but they didn't seem too impressed. They wanted to know where I'd gone after the hockey game. I told them Nina Kong had taken me down to the Monkey's Paw in her limo. This brought a raised eyebrow from Fox but the expression on Cooperman's face remained about the same. Sheer malice.

Cooperman put one foot on the coffee table. His eyes were doing a burn that looked quite a few degrees hotter than my cigar in the ashtray. I picked up the cigar, and probably would have puffed on it, but Fox brought his arm down hard on my wrist and knocked the cigar to the floor. He ground it out with his foot into the beige-colored carpet. It didn't look like something you'd see in *Better Homes and Gardens*.

'Good way to get foot cancer,' I said.

'Who did you talk to at the Monkey's Paw?' he asked. Here was another problem.

The Weasel would be too frightened to talk to the police. He'd never go for it. He'd almost certainly deny he even knew me. He wouldn't give me an alibi if my life depended on it. Of course, it didn't yet but the way things were going, who knew?

And if The Weasel part of my alibi was bad, the Rambam part of it was worse. Given Rambam's background and the nature of the little job we'd both done the night before, I didn't want these guys to touch Rambam with a barge pole. No sir. If they even found out I'd had a Bistro Burger with the lad, they'd pull us both in for a lot more than twenty questions.

'So who did you talk to last night? Did you take a long walk in Sheridan Square Park?' This park was only about ten feet wide and it wasn't much longer than General Sheridan's nose.

The air in the room was getting stale and so was the conversation.

'Let's see if we have this,' said Fox. 'From the time you entered the Monkey's Paw last night until about ten-fifteen this morning when you entered this apartment, no one saw you or spoke to you who might remember you. Right?'

'Right.'

'No alibi?'

'No alibi.' From where I sat I could see the assistant medical examiner in the bedroom. He was crouching on the floor looking very closely at Darlene Rigby's neck. 'Hey!' he shouted, without looking up from his work. 'Who won that Ranger game?'

'Islanders, five to three,' I said.

'It's a shame,' he said.

I was beginning to wonder who I was going to have to screw to keep out of this movie, when they finally let me go. 'We'll keep in touch,' Cooperman said with a very sick little smirk. I wasn't looking too closely, though, because my eyes were already on the door. I figure I got home just a little bit before the stiff got to the morgue.

When you can't win a race with a stiff, you're in trouble.

At the loft there was a message on the machine from Wolf Nachman. I called him back right away.

'What's up, Wolf?' I asked.

'Great news,' he said. 'I've been trying to reach you all morning.'

'What?'

'They sprung McGovern last night,' he said.

## 16

It was a rainy Saturday afternoon in the Village. I was one hockey game and one stiff older and I was watching a Federal Express truck pull into Vandam Street from Greenwich Avenue. The radio station that wanted me to give them twenty-two minutes so they could give me the world had said that it would rain all weekend. That gave me plenty of time to watch.

Rain always made me think of people I wasn't with. Would never be with except when it rained. All my friends today, it seemed, were either dead, born again, or vegetarians. I felt much closer to the dead ones. They always seemed more alive.

The guy with the Federal Express truck was stopping in front of my building. I was thinking of my old friend Slim. Once, a long time ago, some people were giving him grief about his cats knocking over their garbage cans. 'Why are your cats always going into our garbage cans?' they'd said. If I live to be thirty-seven, I'll never forget what old Slim told them. 'They wants to see the world,' he'd said.

The guy was getting out of the Federal Express truck and walking around to the back of it.

I didn't really want to see the world like Slim's cats did, but the way this case was dragging on, I might have to. Two rather bizarre killings in the space of a week. I'd been on the scene before the police both times, and the only thing I'd been able to pick up out of the whole deal had been a shot glass of Jameson.

Maybe I was being too hard on myself. The papers were playing the two murders for all they were worth, which was saying something in a city where murder was almost as commonplace as pastrami.

Even from the limited information they had, the press already saw a fine Italian hand in both crimes. The police were still trying to see a clumsy Irish one. If only the cops and I could somehow pool our information. That didn't seem too likely, but it was essential to finding the killer.

I was looking out at the rain and seeing nothing or everything and whatever people are supposed to see when they look at the rain. The Federal Express guy was looking at a scrap of paper. Then he was waving up at me.

It was too wet for the parachute and the driver was blacker than the puppet so I took the freight elevator down and opened the large metal door in front.

'Package for Four-W. Mr Friedman. That you?' he asked.

'This must be my lucky day,' I said. I signed the receipt and took a narrow brown parcel about two feet long back upstairs with me. There was no return address.

I opened the wrapping paper and lifted the top of the narrow box. It was a pink rose. Attached there was a little white card with a typewritten poem. It read:

I was pinning the rose to my hunting vest when the phones rang. It was 12.37 p.m. and Cynthia was on the line.

'Have you seen McGovern?' she asked.

'Never could see McGovern,' I said. 'He's been on the loose since Wednesday night. Hasn't he been home?'

'No,' she sobbed. This was terrific. 'The police have been here and called several times. They're looking for him too.'

'Well, he's probably out getting completely monstered in one of the bars he hasn't been eighty-sixed from yet. That narrows it down a bit. Maybe I can find him.'

Three days was nothing for a McGovern binge. 'You will call if you find him?' she asked.

'Of course, and you call me if you hear from him first.'

She was really holding up pretty well. In spite of my inherent dislike for all blond men, women and children, I had to admit that Cynthia was growing in my esteem.

McGovern, on the other hand, was running about par for the course.

It looked like it might be time to organize the Village Irregulars and go on a little pub-crawling assignment. But first there were a few loose ends to clear up. I fished the florist's receipt out of the cat-litter tray with a spatula from the kitchen. I didn't cook much anyway. I took the receipt out of the envelope, which was a bit soggy, sprinkled a little Old Spice on it, and put it in the inside pocket of my hunting vest. Then I called the cops.

## 17

It was raining like hell. Maybe worse. There wasn't a cab to be found on Hudson Street, so I walked in the rain to the Sixth Precinct.

Rain was a lot like vomiting. One of the few great equalizers in life. It soaked society dames and bag ladies. People and pigeons. Cops and robbers. It was probably even raining on McGovern. Wherever he was.

Fox and Cooperman were next door to civil, which was about as friendly as they ever got. They were as much at sea as I was but they didn't believe in sharing lifeboats. My only chance was to act as if I knew something.

'Somebody's sending me flowers,' I said. 'One long-stemmed pink rose to be exact.' I took off my coat and patted the flower on my vest.

'Goes nice with your eyes. Sit down, pal,' said Fox. I put the card with the little typewritten poem on the desk and I sat down. Fox brought out a bottle of Old Overholt and a couple of glasses and he poured me a shot. It went down hard but it cut the phlegm pretty good.

When I got my voice back I said: 'The flower and the card arrived at twelve-thirty-five this afternoon. Federal Express. Can you check it out?'

He nodded. He studied the card. 'We'll keep this if you don't mind.'

'You might also check out the fact that Barry Campbell sent those flowers to Frank Worthington.'

'You don't say,' said Cooperman. 'How'd you learn that if you don't mind my asking? You fat-arm the florist?'

'No. I found this receipt the other day in the hallway as I was leaving. It's from the little flower shop around the corner from Worthington's. I called the place and the girl came up with Barry Campbell's name in the ledger. Anything else on Darlene Rigby?' I laid the pink receipt on the desk.

Cooperman looked at the receipt. Then he looked at Fox. Fox looked at the receipt. Then Fox said: 'She was strangled. Trachea crushed . . . leg broken . . . Autopsy shows apparent rape. . . . No traces of semen however . . . Last two calls she made to you at seven-five p.m. and to Peter Myers at almost midnight. . . . She was killed sometime between two and three in the morning. That's the story, bud.'

It wasn't a very pretty one but that was one of the problems with nonfiction. I shook hands with Cooperman and Fox and had almost made the door when Fox brought me up sharp.

'Hold the weddin', pal,' he said. 'If you should hear from your friend McGovern, we want to talk to him yesterday. Get my meaning?'

I said I got his meaning and I left. It was raining harder, if anything, and there were still no cabs. I ducked into a little bar on Christopher to get out of the rain and to call Cynthia. I put in my two bits and listened to the phone ring at McGovern's apartment. I turned around to look at the bar and saw about thirty men making cocktail chatter and watching the rain. I wondered if they saw what I saw when they looked at the rain. Probably.

'Oh, I'm so glad you called,' said Cynthia. This may not have been the first transatlantic phone call but it was definitely the first heterosexual phone call this place had ever known.

'Where are you calling from?' she asked.

'A charming little place called Boots and Saddles, honey; remind me to bring you here sometime. You'd like the ambience. Where's McGovern?'

'I don't know,' she said. 'I'm getting worried.'

'Well, don't,' I said. 'We'll find him tonight. I promise.' It looked like I was going to have to get on the blower and organize the Village Irregulars after all. It also looked like it was going to be one hell of a great night for a good ghost story.

A few of the guys in the bar waved, I waved back, and then walked outside into the rain. 'Come again,' somebody called after me.

Good luck, pal.

The cat was glad to see me and I was glad to see the cat. 'You're the only normal person I've met today,' I told her. I made an espresso and was opening the mail with my Smith & Wesson knife when the phones rang. It was now 4.47 p.m. 'Start talking,' I said.

'Yeah, I'll start talking. This is Detective Sergeant Cooperman. From the Sixth Precinct. Special Crimes Task Force. Remember me?'

'Let me see,' I said. 'Rather tall, Norwegian chap, very elegantly attired.'

'Cut it,' he said. 'What kind of building do you think might have a lot of typewriters in it? I'll answer: a newspaper building. Whose typewriter do you think all three of those little white death notes were typed on?'

'You're kidding,' I said.

'Yeah, I'm kidding. We're putting out an APB on McGovern. You better hope you find him before we do. I'm finished talking.' The line went dead in my hand. For a couple of gumshoes, these guys worked pretty fast.

## 18

The Village has many faces on Saturday night. None of them are too terribly pretty but nobody looks too close. In a notorious chicken-hawk bar on Tenth Street off Seventh Avenue, an older man who looks like the pastor of some small-town church picks up a thirteen-year-old boy. In a shooting gallery on Cornelia Street, you can get any hard drug you want if you can fight your way through the bloody syringes and the wall-to-wall weirdos. I sat on a couch there once for nearly an hour before it finally moved.

About the only thing you won't see in the Village is a man dancing with his wife. If you want to see that you're pretty sick. Probably a voyeur. In New York people may be jaded, jaundiced, superficial, and lifeless, but they still like to see and be seen. It's as normal as apple strudel.

So that's what I was doing on this particular Saturday night. I was going somewhere on my way to see and be seen. Place called the Blue Canary. I was hoping to see and be seen by Barry

Campbell. Somebody knew something and it might as well be him.

Somebody had croaked Frank Worthington and silenced Darlene Rigby before she could open her snapper. Somebody who had at least limited access to McGovern's apartment and to the National Desk of the *Daily News*. Someone who was thorough, imaginative, meticulous, totally ruthless. Someone who was not on the same wavelength as the rest of us. The flesh was slowly beginning to materialize around the grinning Halloween skeleton. But I had an ugly notion that the killer wasn't about to put a sock on it yet. In fact, I was pretty sure of one thing: Whoever this madman was, he was enjoying himself.

Or should I say 'madperson'? When you're dealing with murder, it hardly pays to be a chauvinist.

I beat out a young couple for a cab and took it to Fifty-second Street at Ninth Avenue. When I got there, there was still a line of idiots reaching all the way around the corner, braving the drizzle and hoping to be among the few chosen to gain admittance to the city of light.

Well, they knew what they were doing. They'd come all the way from New Jersey; I hoped they knew what they were doing. True New Yorkers would stand in line only at the Carnegie Delicatessen. Or the lottery. Or the soup kitchen on the Bowery.

In New York you've got to know somebody. Or at least you've got to know somebody who knows somebody. I knew somebody who knew somebody and I'd called him that afternoon, so when I walked up to the front of the line and gave my name to a guy who was about four feet wide, he caved right in and unsnapped the purple velvet rope across the sidewalk. I walked in, the envy of several hundred rain-soaked people.

If this kind of thing really made you start to feel smug, you probably needed a personality transplant.

Normally, I wouldn't have gone into one of these places at gunpoint. But tonight was different. Time was running out for McGovern.

And a homicidal maniac was running loose, very probably preparing to strike again. And if there's one thing worse than a homicidal maniac, it's a homicidal maniac with a sick sense of humor.

The place was an ornate, loud, standard, degenerate disco with lights flashing everywhere in such a way that you couldn't see where you were walking. About five hundred people appeared to be frantically dancing with themselves.

All the employees, men and women alike, wore mannequinlike unisexual tuxedo outfits and looked a little too good. They also looked a little bored, and you really couldn't blame them because anybody that crawled around in a place like that for more than five minutes ought to be bored.

I ordered a beer for five bucks and it was flatter than your little sister, but I couldn't complain because the noise level was about the same as inside a washing machine. I sipped the beer and tried to see where the hell I was going. I kept bumping into people but I didn't know any of them and I didn't want to. I didn't even want to be there. I wished I was outside waiting in line. But it's harder to get out of one of those places than it is to get into one.

I turned a corner and entered another large, crowded room. On the ceiling I could see what looked like light reflected off water. It turned out to be a large swimming pool with a crowd gathered around it. Although I had hoped to find Barry Campbell hanging around somewhere, I didn't think I'd be finding him hanging around quite so literally.

He was suspended from a series of wires attached to the ceiling, and he was going through a series of movements that resembled more than anything else the actions of an emotionally-ill ballet dancer. I couldn't be absolutely certain it was Campbell because of what he was and wasn't wearing, but the more I thought about it, who else could it be?

He was dressed as a mermaid. From head to tail.

He looked like a woman and he looked like a fish, but unfortunately, he still looked like Campbell. It wasn't the kind of thing you'd want to see before you had your kippers and toast. It wasn't even real nice right now. The crowd loved it. And 'it' was certainly what it looked like. Whatever medication this crowd was on, I was going to need a double dose.

I went over to the cute little poolside bar and ordered an eight-dollar shot of Jack Daniel's. It went down faster than some of the people in the Blue Canary, so I ordered another one.

Eventually the show was over, and although many in the crowd continued to stare at the now empty swimming pool, Campbell swung over to the side and slithered through the throng. He disappeared through a side door. I waited a discreet moment or two and then followed. Nobody tried to stop me, which was fortunate because I didn't know the password unless it was 'Get out of my way or I'll kill you and chop you up and put you in the trunk of my Trans-Am.'

I walked down a soundproofed hallway, which came to an end at a closed door. It said PRIVATE – KEEP OUT, but I knew it didn't mean me. I turned the knob and pushed and the door opened into a dimly lit, posh sort of office. It looked a bit too swank for Campbell. Most places did. There he was though, still slightly phosphorescent, sitting on a large settee in one corner bending nose first over some kind of alabaster tabletop. He didn't see me come into the room but that was understandable.

'I didn't recognize you at first,' I said, 'without your wig and tail.'

He jumped higher than a porpoise.

'You ever think about taking that act on the road?' I said.

'What do you want, man?' he said.

'I want to know why you sent Frank Worthington eleven roses,' I said.

'You've made one of the biggest mistakes of your life coming back here, friend,' he said.

'Probably,' I said.

'Security,' he shrilled. 'Security.'

Two guys came into the room. One was wearing a pair of sunglasses and the other was wearing a big, sick, but eager smile. The next thing I knew he was holding a .45 caliber Colt automatic in his left hand.

'Another lefty,' I said.

'Turn around, Slick,' he said.

I turned around and saw Barry Campbell's shy little smile of relief. I think he winked at me, but I couldn't be sure because I pitched forward behind a shattering blow to the back of my head that seared right through whatever the guy had left me of my brain. For a split second every fiber of my body was on fire and the whole world looked like a bad light show at the Fillmore East.

## 19

I woke up on Fifty-first Street next to a guy selling pretzels from a cart. It was morning, my head was throbbing like hell, I ached all over, and I was freezing to death. Too bad some kids hadn't come by and set my coat on fire. I felt like a used-up whore.

My wallet was gone, but I still had most of my teeth and, more important, my change, so I staggered to the corner pay phone and called Ratso. In New York you've got to know somebody.

Ratso said he'd be right over and I said I wasn't going anywhere. 'I had a little hunting accident,' I said. 'I'll be the guy lying by the pretzel cart on Fifty-first Street.' I went back to the cart and waited.

'Jesus,' said Ratso, when he got there. 'You look like you just went ten rounds with Richard Speck. You all right?'

'Just get me back to my cat,' I said, as Ratso bought a pretzel. He hailed a cab, we got in it, and moments later we were hurtling down Ninth Avenue toward the Village. The driver made a point of running every red light and hitting every pothole in the street. There are no Sunday drivers in New York.

Twenty minutes later Ratso and I were sitting at the kitchen table at 199B Vandam. He was pouring us both a second shot of Jameson. The second shot cleared my eyes but didn't do anything for the lump on my head.

It was 10.00 a.m. and everything was pretty quiet on Vandam. The street was a major staging area for garbage trucks, but fortunately for my maltreated medulla, Sunday was their day of rest. It was so quiet you could hear the cockroaches. 'It's a good thing there aren't any goddamn churches around here,' I said. I was hearing more bells and sirens right now in my head than you ever heard on the streets.

Ratso had brought a copy of the *Daily News* and was poring over the hockey standings when a story in another section caught my eye. The headline read: DIARY OF A MURDER SUSPECT: PART I. The by-line was McGovern's and it wasn't in the funnies section either.

My eyes were beginning to blur so I pushed the section across the table and said: 'Ratso, here's an article I think you might enjoy. Maybe you'll be kind enough to read it to me.'

'Uh-hmn,' he said. ' "The *Daily News* in the interest of our readers today begins a five-part series sent to us by secret courier: Diary of a Murder Suspect. The author is a reporter for our National Bureau and is currently a fugitive, wanted by the police in connection with a murder in the Village on February 17. Without our freedom of the press and without the inherent right of a man's innocence until proven guilty, this series would not be possible. . . ." '

'Without our sense of circulation is more like it,' I muttered. 'Well, at least McGovern's alive.'

'Yeah,' said Ratso. 'Our fugitive reporter is probably holed up right now at the Plaza. We'll never find him.'

'We'll find him,' I said. 'We'll find him. In the meantime, see if you can find a large ice pack, will you?'

Ratso found an ice pack and I found my head and put the ice pack on the top of it. I was becoming increasingly aware that if we did not find McGovern soon, his ass was going to belong to the gypsies. If he was lucky.

Ratso had gone home, I'd given the cat a double order of tuna, and I was sacking out for a couple of hours. Taking a little power nap and trying not to dream. It was around two o'clock. I wasn't in the habit of logging incoming calls when I was on the nod, so I didn't know the exact time Nina rang. But I do remember exactly what her first words to me were.

'I remember something,' she said. I thought better of asking her if it would keep until morning.

'It's not too smart to say that around here,' I told her. 'Could get you croaked.'

'You sound terrible,' she said. She sounded good.

'Are you all right?' She was really worried.

'I'm fine,' I said. 'I just came down with a bad case of lockjaw on the way to Fire Island.' I was sitting up now and someone had apparently shut down the steam drill in my head.

'Do you want me to come over?' she asked.

'That would be nice,' I said. We hung up and I glanced around, thinking maybe to straighten up the place a little bit. It didn't really need much straightening up or else it needed a lot. It depended on how you looked at it. I made the bed and threw out a few empty liquor bottles that were on the table. I set the time right on my cuckoo clock from Leningrad that my friend Boris had given me. It didn't keep the time and the cuckoo part didn't work but it came from Leningrad. Come to think of it, Boris didn't work too much either but he might come in handy yet. He had been a combat karate expert in Russia before he saw the light on the Statue of Liberty. He could kill a man in more than a hundred different ways without leaving any marks.

McGovern and I had taken karate lessons twice a week from Boris in his SoHo studio before somebody'd croaked Frank Worthington. I hadn't got to the lesson yet about how to stop a speeding bullet fired at you by a speeding bullethead. Boris probably knew, though. I warned him never to join the army because if he ever had to salute, he'd probably kill himself. He didn't think that was very funny, but Russians never think that anything is very funny. And they're probably right. Anyway, the clock was a piece of crap but I tried to keep it running. Greenwich Village Meantime, at least. I took the rose from my old hunting vest, put it in a vase on the table, and gave it some water. I could have used a drink myself but it didn't feel like Miller Time. I was chasing a few cockroaches off the cupboard when I heard Nina calling from the street. I threw the puppet head down with the parachute and turned on the espresso machine while I waited for her to climb the three flights of stairs. Even without my bird book and binoculars, she'd looked pretty good standing on the sidewalk.

She looked even better standing at the door. She put her arms around me. 'Gently,' I said. I didn't have to tell her. Some people just have the touch. She felt great.

'Why don't you lie down on the couch,' she said. Her hair was cut after the fashion of a little French newsboy. I didn't go for little French newsboys but it looked good on her. I could imagine a number of things that would look good on her. One of them was myself. I walked over to the couch and I lay down.

Nina was giving me a pretty fair impersonation of a massage when the phones range. 'I'll get it,' she said. I didn't log that one either, but I just lay there on the couch thinking about logging something else. 'It's Cynthia,' she said.

'Tell her I'll meet her at five p.m. at McGovern's.'

'You're very popular,' she said when she returned.

'Yeah. Look, be very careful what you say if you call me on that phone. I'll lay odds it's tapped, along with McGovern's, and the police'll probably be along to have a little talk with you as well, so just be careful. Somebody's croaked Frank and somebody's croaked Darlene and somebody might just try to croak somebody else.'

'I'm very careful,' she said. 'How does this feel?'

'Better than the out-call service from *Screw* magazine,' I said. She wasn't all that good at it but she didn't have to be. 'What were you going to tell me?' I asked.

'Well, this was about a year and a half ago. One day I was walking with Frank down Fourth Street, and he pointed off to his right toward that block off Charles Street.'

'Did he think he was on a Gray Line Tour?'

'No, he didn't. He said, "That's where my shrink lives." '

'He didn't say anything else?'

'That was it. "That's where my shrink lives." I'm not sure which side of the street or anything, just Charles to the right of Fourth as you're walking east.'

'I'll give that shrink a good checkup from the neck up,' I said. 'I wonder if he drives a Mercedes and smokes a pipe and has a large dog.'

'He could also drive a station wagon,' she said. She was working on my head while she was working on my head. I noticed she had a nice little laugh and she knew how to use it. She even knew when to use it. I'd always believed that if you could make a woman laugh you could take her to bed with you.

'Who sent you the rose?' she asked a little too casually.

'That's what we're going to find out. Go easy on my head,' I said, touching the lump on top of it. 'That's where my shrink lives.'

Nina took my hand and held it over her left breast. She didn't really have to hold it but she did. 'That's where my shrink lives,' she whispered.

I didn't doubt it.

## 20

By the time I got to Jane Street to see Cynthia, I was feeling remarkably better than I had that morning. Not only were Nina and I getting better acquainted, but I had a much clearer sense of which leads I might want to pursue. I had been treading a tortuous and confused path along which the killer had left seemingly no real clues to his identity. Now, for the first time, I could see a few careless footprints in the clay, and a bent twig or two along the trail, like the twisted synapses of the bent mind I was chasing.

On a Blue Canary cocktail napkin, I had made a little list of what I had to do. It read as follows: (1) Find Barry Campbell, turn him upside down, and use the point of his head to pick up paper with. Also check out the flowers he'd sent to Frank Worthington. (2) Grill Pete Myers to see if he knew about anything besides the British Knish. (3) Check the *Daily News* building's National Desk for access to McGovern's typewriter; check the newspaper morgue for old McGovern by-lines over the years. To this, I added number (4) Find Frank Worthington's shrink and get some insights into whatever you prefer to call the mind of a stiff.

This last might require my giving the shrink a healthy jolt of shock therapy, but I liked shrinks only a little better than I liked lawyers, so I wasn't going to worry about it.

I put the cocktail napkin away, pulled a cigar out of my hunting vest, and rang the buzzer of 2B. I lighted the cigar and, satisfying Cynthia that I wasn't Tex Watson, pushed the door open as she buzzed me in. Actually, security of this kind almost never worked. The buzzers, alarms, and chains on the door worked fine. The problem was that no one ever really knew who Tex Watson was until he presented his card. And by that time, it was too late.

On the second floor, I noticed a young couple coming out of Frank Worthington's old place with a little baby in a pram. About the only thing they don't waste time with in New York is renting your apartment once you fall through the trapdoor. They're interviewing new prospects before you even have time to wake up in hell. You go down; the rent goes up.

'Hi, Cynthia,' I said.

'Come on in,' she said, as she took the chain off the door.

I looked around inside the apartment. She wasn't going to win any housekeeping awards, but the place looked tidier than when McGovern had been there. Of course, the three little pigs probably could've done a better job than McGovern.

I had located some cognac and was searching the kitchen cabinet for an appropriately stemmed glass when I noticed a little white snow seal winking at me from one corner. McGovern never used cocaine, though he used just about everything else.

'Been to see our friend Adrian, I see.'

'She came by last night. You must think I'm terrible.'

'Yeah, I'm all for clean living,' I said. 'My body is a temple where I go to pray for drugs.' I heard a wrong chord somewhere in my mind but I wasn't sure what it was or who was playing it.

'Look,' I said, 'McGovern's bound to get in touch with one of us very soon, so we've got to keep in touch. He's probably sorting things out and he's obviously being very careful.'

'But why hasn't he called?'

'I just told you, Cynthia. He's being careful. Hasn't it crossed your desk that your phones are being monitored by the police, both here and at your own place? Where do you live?'

'New Jersey,' New Jersey was my second favorite place. My first was everywhere else. 'Like a drink?'

She shook her head. I was a big enough phony to get by in situations with depressed, distraught women, but that still didn't make it my idea of a good time.

'You see, honey, McGovern is still the number-one suspect in this affair. If you speak to him and don't report it to the police, you're an accessory to the crime. Speaking of which, I want you to be very careful on this phone in general and especially when you're talking to me. Believe me, the cops are watching, listening, and waiting for McGovern to show himself. But he'll find a way of making contact with us, don't worry.'

Actually, I was starting to get pretty worried. Why hadn't McGovern found a way of getting in touch with one of us? Maybe he was busily plotting to rub us both out. It happens. In fact, it happens about as often as it doesn't happen. Amazingly few premeditated murders ever involve strangers or casual acquaintances. You have to get to know somebody pretty well before you decide to murder them.

As I left Cynthia's place, something was bothering me but I didn't quite know what the hell it was. She didn't hug me, but she squeezed my hand a few times instead. I could live with it. Something else seemed to be bothering Cynthia besides McGovern. I couldn't even guess what it was. I didn't even know what was bothering me.

I figured I'd draw a bye on seeing Adrian this trip. One dizzy dame was enough for a Sunday afternoon, and I doubted that there would be an appreciable amount of progress in the stained-glass department.

Meanwhile, I was still feeling somewhat in the debit column in the gray matter department. I could've written volumes on what I didn't know if I'd only known what it was. Trouble was, I didn't. I only knew I'd better find the killer before the noose tightened forever around McGovern's seventeen-and-a-half-inch neck.

## 21

It was about ten o'clock on Sunday night. The weather had become increasingly colder, but at least the rain had stopped earlier in the evening. Charles Street was still there. So was Frank Worthington's shrink, whoever he was.

It was a beautiful street with elegant brownstones and quaint little cafés. If you had to be a shrink and you had to live in the Village, this was the place. It even had what New Yorkers like to think of as trees struggling along here and there up through the sidewalks. But they weren't the kind of trees that would ever prevent you from seeing the forest. It was there. And it was at least as dark as *The Jungle Book*.

I combed the two blocks of Charles Street nearest to Fourth Street for the better part of two hours, weeding out the handful of dentists and the occasional proctologist until I came up with three possible shrinks. It was a nerveracking procedure because many of the little bronze plates were deliberately vague, only saying something like Dr Stanley Livingstone and requiring my calling up on the intercom to determine the doctor's area of expertise.

I talked to baby-sitters, wives, and housekeepers, most of whom grudgingly gave me a little information and all of whom were ticked off about the late hour. It was a good thing I didn't need a doctor.

I thought of what Albert Einstein's maid had once reportedly told a guy who called up asking if the doctor made house calls. She'd told him: 'He's not the kind of doctor who does nobody no good.'

By the time I had my three possibles, I felt like a Jehovah's Witness with a rejection complex. Of the three shrinks living in that section of Charles Street, one was dead and one was at a shrinks' convention in Los Angeles. I didn't know which was worse.

The other one was my boy. Dr Norman Bock. It was 11.45 p.m.

What the hell. I wasn't here for my health. I pushed the button.

A deep, resonant voice laced with thinly veiled irritation said: 'Yes.'

'Dr Bock?'

'Yes. Are you aware of what time it is?' He was warming up to me a little.

'Yes, Doctor. I'm sorry it's so late but my name is Marvin Barenblatt and I'm having an anxiety attack.' I tried to sound as miserable as I felt.

'How did you get my name and address?' he asked. He sounded thoroughly disgusted with life on this planet. He didn't know it, but he had a ways to go to catch up with me. If I'd had my way, I would've given both of us a kick in the ass.

'I got your name from Frank Worthington, a former patient of yours.' He was certainly that.

'Hmmnn,' he said. He did a pretty nice job of crowding just a hint of suspicion and just a glint of recognition into that 'hmmnn.' I couldn't tell which way he was going to go. It made me feel kind of vulnerable. That's probably what they taught them in med school these days. They sure weren't boning up on the bedside manner.

'What was your name again?'

'Marvin. Marvin Barenblatt.' I had affected a sort of whiney shrill and I was beginning to feel pretty much at home with it.

'Call me in the morning, Mr Barenblatt. I'll try to squeeze you in in the afternoon.'

I whined a little 'Good night, Dr Bock' into the intercom, but he'd already gone off to ritually floss his teeth. Well, I'd see him in his office tomorrow.

The human mind was a funny thing, and I was betting my life that Frank Worthington's file, once I got my hands on it, was going to crack us all up.

When I got home it was after midnight. The cat wasn't too happy about how long I'd been gone and neither was I. When you have a cat, you assume certain responsibilities that, in a spiritual sense, may transcend those of a marital or a business relationship. We both felt a little let down.

I made some coffee and I poured a cup and I was thinking about having a cigar when the phones rang. It was McGovern. 12.25 a.m.

'This is Lord Baskerville,' he said.

'You dog, you.'

'Look, I'm sorry I haven't gotten in touch.'

'Don't mention it, pal.'

'Listen. You know the one place I haven't been eighty-sixed from in the Village?'

'Yeah.' That was an easy one. The Bistro.

'Well, if you can be there in an hour, I'll call you.'

'Right-ho, Baskerville, old boy. Been a pleasure talking to you.' Less that fifteen seconds. Even phone-company security couldn't trace that one for the cops. I lighted a cigar, fed the cat, put on my hunting vest, and headed out into the night.

It was past one o'clock when I got to the Bistro. It wasn't very crowded for a Sunday night. Maybe that was why they hadn't eighty-sixed McGovern. They needed everybody they could get. Well, they had me tonight.

That was about all they had. Going down the bar, there was one ebony-colored gentleman fighing off the DT's, one recently retired backgammon hustler, one Puerto Rican who looked like a leftover extra from *West Side Story*, one bag lady who'd come in from the cold, and one whatever the hell I was supposed to be.

If you could tell a man by the company he keeps, you couldn't have told me anything.

I ordered a Bistro Burger from my old pal Dave at the bar and I waited to hear from McGovern. 'Drag it through the garden, Dave.'

'Right you are.'

I wondered if I'd miss the Bistro when I was dead. Conceivably. But the older I got, the less likely it seemed. I wasn't going to miss much else either at the rate I was going.

Of course, most people didn't know what they were missing. And they sure didn't know what they weren't missing. Nor did they know that there was any difference between the two.

'That's why everybody else in the world is happy and I'm as lonely as a lighthouse,' I thought.

Of course it wasn't true. It was just something that happened to people who had to wait too long for their Bistro Burgers.

So I ordered a Canadian Mist for a Canadian I missed and I bought a drink for the bag lady. 'Cheers,' I said.

'Mind your manners,' she said.

I was hungry enough to eat pork tartare by the time the Bistro

Burger arrived. And I had all five pounds of it in my hands en route to my choppers when the phone rang. I set the burger down and walked over to the pay phone, which was the only phone in the place and was located in the middle of the room right next to the jukebox. It wasn't very private, but then neither was the men's room at Grand Central Station. And a lot of business was conducted there.

It was McGovern.

'Hey,' he said, 'I've missed you.'

'Yeah, where are you?'

'I've been riding the couch circuit for a while. I'm at Costello's.' Costello's was the drinking newspaperman's bar on Forty-fourth Street. And what newspaperman didn't drink? 'Been staying with Brennan and here and there.' Mick Brennan was a charming, high-powered, wild, and well-connected British free-lance photographer. Two of his many claims to fame were that he'd covered the Falklands War from mainland Argentina, and that he was a personal friend of Michael Caine's. I liked him anyway.

'McGovern, how long can you keep this up before you get nailed?' Hell, for the right money, I was ready to turn him in.

'Hey, I'm making it. Did you read my column today?'

'Yeah, I did, and I'll bet the ranch you'll be back in the sneezer before they can run part five. "Diary of an Idiot." ' McGovern sounded fairly monstered. Couldn't say I blamed him.

'Tell Cynthia I'll drop by and see her at the place one night this week.'

'That's real smart,' I said.

'How's she holding up?'

'About as well as you are. She'll make it. I'm not so sure about you.'

I took a quick look to see if my Bistro Burger was intact. Nobody'd touched it, but I could see the heat disseminating from it with alarming rapidity.

'Do you want me to come up there?' I asked.

'No, I've got to be on the move. You know how it is.'

'Yeah. This fugitive underground journalist thing is going to your head. Better tell me about this goddamn ghost you saw, just in case I never see you again.'

'The ghost. Yeah, the ghost. Look, I didn't tell anybody but you and Cynthia about this.'

'It's a good thing. You tell the cops and you'll wind up in wig city for sure.' I didn't tell him, but that might be better than being sentenced for second-degree murder. Hanging out with guys who thought they were Jesus and Napoleon would probably be preferable to being in a cell with a large black man who called you Louise.

'It was a little while after you'd left and a little before the police came across the hall to my apartment and found the gun. That's when I saw the ghost. It was standing there by the stairs in the hallway, and then it just disappeared.'

'Well, I got two questions for you: Number one is, why didn't the cops see the ghost? And number two is, were you drinking?' Actually, I knew the answer to the second one. It was the same answer you'd expect if you'd asked 'Do fish fart underwater?'

'The cops probably didn't see this ghost because they were busy in Worthington's apartment and also because they weren't looking for this particular ghost.'

'I see. Was the ghost anybody you knew?' This was starting to get good.

'Yes, it was. That's the funny part. I'd had a few drinks, you know, but as drunk as I've ever got, I've never seen a ghost before and I never want to see one again, I can tell you.'

'Well, come on, McGovern, how the hell did you know it was a ghost? This ain't *The Twilight Zone*. I don't have to stand around here all night listening to this crap. How do you know it wasn't somebody in the building going out for a pizza?'

'Because while the cops were in the other apartment with Frank Worthington's body. I saw the ghost in the hall. It was coming right toward me. . . . It was carrying a flower. . . . I know this sounds crazy . . . you're going to hate me for this. . . .'

'Don't worry.' How could anyone hate a large, personable Irishman whose brain was slowly turning to Silly Putty? 'Just tell me how you knew what you saw was a goddamn ghost.'

'Because I knew who it was.'

'Who, then? Who was the ghost?' I was starting to feel a little uneasy in spite of myself.

'It was Frank Worthington,' he said. 'I saw Frank Worthington's ghost in the hall after he was murdered.'

## 22

If my conversation with McGovern hadn't sufficiently taken away my appetite, the figure darkening the door was more than enough to finish the job.

It was Detective Sergeant Cooperman, and he didn't especially look as if he'd been having a good day. That made two of us.

It was what could be described as a close call.

'Who you calling, pal? Fixing up a late date with Greta Garbo?' This guy was funny.

'Yeah,' I said. I drifted over to my Bistro Burger, and Cooperman drifted right with me. He sat down on the other side of me from the bag lady. 'I'd like you to meet a friend of mine,' I said to her, gesturing toward Cooperman.

'Watch it,' she said.

It didn't take a rocket scientist to figure out that Cooperman was running a stakeout on McGovern's place. The question was, what was I doing here?

'What are you doing here, pal?' he asked.

'What am I doing here? I'm a regular. I'm always here on Sunday night. Right, Dave?'

'Right you are,' said Dave.

I wasn't feeling very hungry, and Cooperman said he was, so in a rare display of brotherhood, he and I decided to split my Bistro Burger between us. He looked up at Dave the bartender. 'You got a knife, pal?' he said.

'Why don't we just use the one in McGovern's back?' I said. Cooperman chuckled at that one.

'Say, your old pal must be getting just a little nervous in the service right about now.'

'I wouldn't know,' I said.

'You haven't talked to him, eh?'

'No.' The hamburger was going down like lead. Cooperman was smiling and chomping away at his half of the burger at the same time. I'd hate to have to watch him eat every night.

'Well, I'm sure he'll turn up pretty soon,' he said. 'Maybe belly up if he isn't careful.' Cooperman was starting to really enjoy himself. It was past time for me to get the hell out of there.

I paid the check, left Dave a good tip, said good night to him, to Cooperman, and to the bag lady, and walked out. I figured that it must be just another one of those wonderful coincidences of life that Cooperman and I had run into each other in that place at that time. Next time I ran into Cooperman, I hoped I'd be driving.

When I got back to 199B Vandam I put on the sarong that I'd got from Borneo, made some camomile tea, drank it, and went to bed. But sleep came slower than a frigid woman.

I played the same hand over and over again in my mind, but the cards just weren't stacking up right. I knew the other players. I knew the odds. But somehow I didn't trust the look in the dealer's eyes.

Anything could happen, and if I knew anything it probably would.

Funny bumping into Cooperman . . .

It was a small world, but I'd hate to paint it.

## 23

When I got up Monday morning I felt like I'd been run over by a bookmobile but otherwise I was fine. It was too early to call the shrink's office for my appointment so I made some coffee and was just starting to look over the score for the Broadway show I was working on when the phones rang. It was 9.07 a.m. Ratso.

'Start talking,' I said.

'Well, I was born in a small Texas town. My family didn't have much money so I went to work at a very early age pumping gas in a whorehouse and then . . .'

'Give it a rest, will you?'

'Sure,' said Ratso. 'Just thought you'd want to know that one of our friends is performing tonight at the Ear Inn. Good ol' Peter Myers.' The Ear was a little bar on Spring Street that went in for literary and artistic endeavors in a big way. The neon *B* in the word *Bar* had burned out in several places and for years had read *Ear* and that's the reason they call the Ear the Ear.

'Knowing our friend,' I said, 'I'm afraid to ask what he's performing. Is it of a sexually explicit nature?' Maybe he was sticking it in his own ear.

'Oh, no,' said Ratso, 'it's quite legitimate. Myers has been on the calendar there for over a month. He's giving a poetry reading. You know, "Gather ye rosebuds while ye may," that kind of thing. Not really your cup of tea probably, but considering he may be trying to kill you, I just thought you might like to attend. It's at eight o'clock tonight.'

The only guy I'd ever want to go hear read poetry was Dylan Thomas and it wasn't bloody likely because he'd been dead for thirty years. At least I hoped he was dead; they buried him thirty years ago. 'Okay, I'll meet you there,' I said.

'Sounds delightful, doesn't it?' said Ratso.

'Sounds pretty goddamn weak to me,' I said and hung up. I had another cup of coffee, lighted my first cigar of the new day, and thought about a lot of things. I even thought about watering the plants but didn't get much further than that. It was time to see if Dr Norman Bock could squeeze me in. When it came time for me to level with this guy, it was probably going to turn pretty ugly.

I picked up the phone. Got a young secretary's voice. 'Doctor's office. May I help you?' she said.

'Marvin Barenblatt here,' I shrilled. 'Dr Bock said he'd try to squeeze me in this afternoon. I'm a new patient.' Poor Marvin.

'Fine, Mr Barenblatt. How does three o'clock sound?'

'Fine,' I told her. And that was that.

I called Cynthia and I called Wolf Nachman to keep them abreast of the situation such as it was. Cynthia sounded like she hadn't slept since I'd seen her last. Wolf sounded the way all lawyers sound – like life never quite touches them. Maybe lawyers just never have any personal problems of their own. They just spend their lives giving gray hair to other people.

It was now five days since somebody had torpedoed Darlene Rigby's career. It was ten days since somebody had snuffed Worthington. He hadn't even had a career to torpedo, but they'd croaked him just the same. Obviously Worthington was croaked for a deeply personal reason, one which Darlene Rigby had apparently been privy to. She had known something and it had been something that hadn't kept till the morning.

No murderer could be said to be truly sane but there was always a reason, real or imagined, for a killer to kill. This killer struck me as rational, methodical, and lucky, but he was pushing his luck. All I could really do was try to get an in-depth look at Frank Worthington's mind, and a firmer grasp of where Nina, Campbell, Myers, and Adrian were coming from. And keep my fingers crossed for McGovern. Get out my lucky shamrock for the boy. God knows he was going to need it.

Two-thirty on an unseasonably mild Monday afternoon found me walking Marvin Barenblatt's sick brain down Fourth Street on its way to his psychiatrist's office. I was whistling a tune. It was a tune from an old Broadway show and it was jarred only occasionally by some teenage idiot with a ghetto blaster or by the honking of traffic behind a car that was hopeless lost in that Ariadne's maze that is the Village.

An obsidian young man flew by backward on a skateboard. A homosexual couple was patching up an argument on the corner. One was holding the other to his chest, stroking his head. It looked like spring was just around the corner.

I didn't care what a young man's fancy turned to in spring. My mind was on murder. Two murders to be exact. And this was going to be a long winter. Even Marvin knew that the appearance of spring in New York was phonier than a French waiter. And Marvin was a phony himself.

I put murder on the back burner and stopped whistling when I reached Dr Norman Bock's office on Charles Street. If Marvin had a problem, so did I.

Being Marvin Barenblatt at all was a nauseating experience and about another five or ten minutes was all that I was going to be good for. I'd always made it a policy of intensely disliking anyone named Marvin. Now I knew why. Marvin was getting on my nerves. I couldn't wait for him to meet Dr Bock and leave me alone.

I pushed the buzzer, the little voice said, 'Doctor's office,' and I said: 'Marvin Barenblatt here to see Dr Bock.' I gained entry.

The little voice that had said 'Doctor's office' was sitting behind a desk in a container that must have weighed in at two hundred pounds. Only a shrink or an undertaker could have afforded to have a receptionist as wide as her desk. And for a fat lady, she wasn't all that friendly. Neither was I. Fortunately, neither of us had to wait too long.

Bock opened the door into the waiting room and said, 'Mr Barenblatt.' The receptionist said, 'You can go in now,' which was a little unnecessary because I was already going in. I shot her my best Marvin look of cloying reproach, but she only looked at me with pity in her eyes. I followed Bock into his pastel basement shrinking parlor and walked around a bit looking at the abstract crap on the wall that somebody'd seen fit to frame. If it wasn't the work of his patients, it should have been.

'I feel like I know you already, Marvin,' he said.

'Yeah. Sorry about last night, Doctor.'

'Oh, don't worry about it. That's what we're here for.'

'Beautiful day out there today, isn't it?' It was hard to tell if you lived in a pastel basement. Molten lava could've been coming down Charles Street and he wouldn't have known it.

'Yes. I'd say it was spring if I didn't know better,' he said. 'Well, what seems to be bothering you, Marvin? You started to tell me last night, I believe.'

'Yeah. Sorry about that, Doc.' I thought I'd start to repeat myself a time or two. Might be worth a jot on a pad.

'Don't mention it,' he said, a little curtly, I thought. I'd seen better eye contact in drunks.

'Have you been in touch with Frank Worthington lately?' I asked.

'No. I haven't seen Frank in several years now. How's he doing?'

'Not too well,' I said.

'That's a shame. Does pipe smoking bother you?'

'Not at all. I like it, in fact. It reminds me of my old Granddad Barenblatt. He used to smoke a big old briar pipe. Do you have a dog?'

'Yes, I do,' he laughed. 'Why do you ask?'

'You look like a dog lover.'

'Do you have a dog, Marv?'

'No, I have a cat.' At a hundred and twenty-seven dollars an hour somebody was getting hosed.

'Cats are nice, I understand,' he said.

'They can be a lot of trouble sometimes.'

'So can dogs, here in the city,' he said. Of course, anything was a problem here in the city. The care and upkeep of a ball-point pen could be a problem. This was going nowhere pretty quickly. Time to put some cards on the table. Assuming that this guy could really shrink a head, mine was going to be about the size of a LeSueur pea before I learned anything useful about Frank Worthington.

'Look, Doc,' I said, 'there's a few things I ought to tell you before this goes too far.'

'What's on your mind, Marv?'

'Well, for one thing, someone's threatening to kill me.'

'Okay, Marv.' He really believed that one.

'For another, while Marvin Barenblatt is a very melodic name, it's not mine.' Bock sat up straight and put down his pipe. He seemed to be running down a few deep-breathing exercises.

'What name would you like to use?' he asked finally.

'I'd like to use the name Frank Worthington,' I said. 'He won't be needing it anymore. Somebody croaked him eleven days ago. That's why he's not doing too well. I'm working unofficially but I am in touch with the cops in charge of the case. Can I see his file?'

'Out of the question,' said Bock hotly. I got up and walked over to his desk. 'Especially,' he said, 'after the totally fraudulent way in which you've presented yourself.'

'Now, Doc, don't let old Marvin get your goat. I thought he was a woosie of the first water myself, but you'll find that I'm not and I want to know all there is to know about Frank Worthington two years ago. What were his problems? Was the boy out where the buses don't run? I mean, had the date on his carton expired, or what?'

Bock just screwed up his mouth and shook his head. He started to light his pipe. I took out a cigar and fired it up and waited.

'Frank Worthington . . .' said the shrink softly. A dreamy sort of expression came into Bock's eyes. Dreamy and maybe something else. Even psychiatrists had their dreams. And their secrets.

'Frank Worthington was a man of great physical beauty,' he said. 'He was attractive to many women. And to many men. He seemed almost to drift through life like a fragile and beautiful butterfly just beyond everybody's reach. People saw him and they wanted to . . . they wanted to . . . to collect him . . . but nobody ever could. . . .'

At this point Bock stopped to relight his pipe. Then he looked right at me and said in an almost wistful voice: 'Nobody ever could. . . .'

'Looks to me like somebody pinned his wings pretty good, Doc,' I said.

'I'm going out of town Wednesday,' he said brusquely, 'and my schedule is really very crowded. So I'll have to ask you to please leave now, Mr Barenblatt. Immediately.' He stood up abruptly, walked across the room, opened the door, and held it for me.

My appointment was obviously over.

Wednesday night, however, I planned to be back with Rambam and his little putty knife. But I could see that getting into Frank Worthington's head was going to be a lot bigger operation than getting into Frank Worthington's apartment.

Dr Bock nodded curtly at me as I walked by him into the waiting room, then he disappeared into his office, closing the door behind him. I walked past the receptionist who stared at me with disgust.

'For the initial evaluation, sir,' she said, 'we charge . . .'

'Bill me,' I said.

## 24

I took a cab up to Costello's bar on Forty-fourth to meet Mick Brennan and have him take me over to the *Daily News* building just two blocks away. Mick was at the bar drinking a creative gin-based concoction of his own invention and reading 'The Diary of a Murder Suspect: Part II.'

'McGovern's a bit more out there that I quite thought, mate,' he said. I didn't disagree. When the cops did catch him, they were going to be so mad they'd throw him in the back of the pen.

'Mick, do you have a Minox?'

A Minox was a small Japanese surveillance camera much favored by spies, counterespionage agents, and people who wished to photograph the files of anal-retentive shrinks.

'No, I'll have a Heineken,' he said.

A Heineken was a Dutch beer much favored by Mick Brennan. On occasion, he would favor more than one.

'Mick,' I said, 'I know you only like to plan half an hour ahead, but I have an important assignment for you late Wednesday night that is almost as dangerous, not to say stupid, as it was for a wiseass Brit photographer to be caught hanging around mainland Argentina during the Falklands War. Or should I say skirmish?'

'War,' he said.

'War,' I agreed, and ordered a Bass ale along with a Jameson to keep it company. For nothing in this world looks quite as lonely on a bar as a pint of beer without a shot of Jameson unless it's a shot of Jameson without a chaser.

'Let's drink to war,' I said. 'Peace can be so tedious.'

'Spoken like a man who's never seen one,' said Brennan.

'You participant-observers of life must get a little world-weary sometimes. Can we pencil you in for Wednesday night?'

'Let's drink to penciling me in.'

'To penciling you in.' He joined me in a shot. 'Cheers, mate,' he said.

'Are your sure you'd like to know what I'm penciling you in for?'

'Not particularly. But let's have it before I die of ennui.'

'We're going to break into a shrink's office in the Village and photograph the confidential files of a recent bisexual murder victim. The killer has struck twice now. And he's not very nice. He's still on the loose, you know. Could be me or you. Where were you last Wednesday night?'

'I was visiting your friend Gunner.' Brennan smiled impishly. Brennan said just about everything impishly. When he wanted to be, he could be as bad a troublemaker as Jesus.

'What were you doing over there? Helping her adjust her light meter?'

'Why don't you break into her apartment and photograph her little diary and find out?' he said. When he wasn't being impish, Brennan could get a little testy. If there was one thing I hated, it was a testy Brit. It just didn't wear well on them.

'I'll drink to that,' I said, and we ordered and downed a couple more shots. I wanted to be sure we weren't walking on our knuckles when we left there because I wanted to be fairly sharp when we got to the *Daily News* and however sharp you have to be to attend a poetry reading. I didn't really think a poetry reading would be all that dangerous. In fact, it sounded so exciting I wondered if I could stay awake through it. Which goes to show that the books are filled with stuff I didn't know. But I would be learning. The hard way.

We left Costello's still walking upright and headed over to the *Daily News*.

As my father once remarked when he got back from a trip abroad, 'If you've seen one Sistine Chapel, you've seen 'em all.' That was particularly true of big-city newspaper offices. There is a certain trapped spirit of resigned cynicism that you can catch like a virus if you stay there too long. Probably it was reality. I wouldn't know. But my respect for McGovern grew. To survive as a maverick in the truth business was no mean feat.

One of the first things that grabs you when you walk into the *Daily News* building is the giant blue globe of what we are sometimes pleased to call the planet earth that is sunk into the lobby and is as big as a St Patrick's Day hangover. Emanating from it are mosaic markers on the floor of the lobby to show the various distances away of major cities of the world. If you said that the distances were all measured from Costello's bar, you probably wouldn't be wrong.

Brennan and I circled the globe a couple of times along with a few visitors from Japan and several guys who looked like professional loiterers. A guard kept a wary eye on the group of us. If anyone had been thinking of going to Rome, it was 3,781 miles away. If you wanted to bang your head against the Great Wall of China it was 6,882 miles away in Beijing, but if you couldn't stand to wait that long, you could bang your head against the Wailing Wall, which was only 5,696 miles away in Jerusalem. Or you could just move to Cleveland, which was only 404 miles away but would make you feel like banging your head against a wall. Piccadilly Circus was 3,475 miles away in London and the Moscow Circus, if it hadn't defected yet, was 4,665 miles from here.

The circus that I had to deal with was on the seventh floor.

Brennan and I negotiated the elevator all right but ran into immediate trouble on the seventh floor. The guy at the desk there appeared not to know Brennan from Adam and he looked right through me like I wasn't there.

'You sure this is the lingerie department?' I asked Brennan. He silenced me with a severe glance.

'Is Bob Miller here?' he asked.

'You want to speak to the city editor?' said the guy at the desk. 'Are you kidding? He wouldn't pick up the phone for God.'

Mick maintained his dignity, which is something the British do very well when they want to. They have more of it than they need to start with. 'Tell him Mick Brennan is here to see him.'

Rather grudgingly the guy called the city editor, and before you could have cooked a two-minute egg, the waves were parting, the wheels were turning, the metaphors were mixing, and the two of us were shaking hands with Virgil and following him down into the circles of Hell. Miller led us through a paper-strewn, workaday mazeway of human ratholes, cubicles, and plush offices and into the huge, smoke-filled, bustling city room. As the name implied, it looked like a small city.

'I'd like to have a look at McGovern's typewriter,' I said.

'That's no problem,' said Miller. 'It's one of the few old heirlooms we've got left.' It was true. Everywhere you looked, at almost every desk in the city room, reporters worked with computer screens instead of typewriters. Miller showed us around.

'About seven years ago these buggers started taking over. Video-display terminals. VDTs. Typewriter's practically a dinosaur. Sorry to say it, but it's true. There's McGovern's desk. Where the hell he is, I don't know. Make yourself at home. I'll be back in a few minutes.'

'Nice guy,' I said.

'That's what you think,' said Brennan. 'Even Jesus hates a city editor. And usually for good reasons.'

I was hardly listening to Mick by then. I was looking over McGovern's typewriter. The old dinosaur that had helped the cops hang two murders on him. I knew the city room wasn't humming with action all the time, but it was hard to conceive of someone coming in here on several occasions and using McGovern's machine without someone seeing him. I doubted if the cops had even bothered with that possibility. I wasn't even too sure I believed it myself.

I put a piece of paper into the old Underwood and typed 'break a leg, baby.' Then, under it, I typed 'i'm sending you eleven roses . . . the twelfth rose is you.' I used no caps, just like the original notes to Frank Worthington and Darlene Rigby. Everything the murderer had written was in lowercase letters. 'It's interesting,' I told Brennan, 'and it raises the shocking possibility that the murderer was e. e. cummings.'

'That's cute,' said Mick. 'Better get cracking on whatever it is you're doing because Miller may change his rabbit mind and chuck us out of here at any moment.'

'It was probably the last thing either of them ever read,' I continued, half to myself. They certainly hadn't had time to read the writing on the wall. Well, maybe Darlene had. I felt a small twinge of guilt but it passed quickly.

Every typewriter, especially an old baby like this one, has its own set of fingerprints that it leaves on every typed page. I put the page down under the desk light and Brennan and I pored over it. If I had been Sherlock I could've left the magnifying glass at home. I wasn't even going to need 'gather ye rosebuds while ye may.' The *l* on McGovern's machine was visibly flawed. You could have driven a *Daily News* truck through it without scratching the paint. I was sure of that *l* on Worthington's note, and I remembered it in Darlene's original note and in the poem sent to me. A bit too obvious, but there it was, as they say, in black and white right before my eyes.

No question about it, the notes had been typed, all three of them, on McGovern's Underwood. Also there was no question in my mind that McGovern himself hadn't typed them. Almost no question.

I sent Brennan home and told him to get his equipment and his act together for what could be a fairly nasty Wednesday night. Someone pointed me through a long narrow hallway and I followed it right up to the desk of an old lady who sat guarding the *Daily News* morgue. Nice work if you could get it.

I told her I'd spoken to Bob Miller and I was looking for any and all by-lines by McGovern. Her eyes widened a bit. 'I'll see what I can find,' she said.

'How far does the morgue go back in time?' I asked.

'June of 1919,' she said.

'That was a good year for Château de Cat Piss but it's a bit farther than I want to go. How about going ten years back? Everything by McGovern that you can find.'

'Well, it's all here,' she said. I could see that. I could also see that this would be an exercise in tedium if I couldn't light a rather large bonfire under this nice old lady's ass.

'Ma'am,' I said, 'right now the police are looking frantically for

McGovern and they believe he's a prime murder suspect as you've no doubt read.' She nodded. She might've been nodding off for all I knew, but I continued in a brisker tone.

'Anything and everything by McGovern. We've got to find something that connects up to these murders. It's got to be here somewhere. Okay, let me have it.'

She had some kind of a VDT there too and she stoked it up. As something came onto the screen she'd get that issue off the shelves and toss it on the table for me.

The first thing she came up with was a story by McGovern about six months old and datelined Dallas. PET PYTHON SWALLOWS EIGHT-MONTH-OLD BABY. Nice item.

'Keep 'em coming,' I shouted. She did. An article about five years old concerning Senator Baker's wife going into surgery. It was headlined BAKER'S WIFE UNDER KNIFE.

'No,' I said. I thought of McGovern's attitude toward his profession. He'd summed it up in one sentence: 'I don't do long leads and I don't work in the rain.'

McGovern had felt that there was a built-in cynicism about the newspaper business. If twenty-four Mexicans were killed in a bus wreck, it was worth a short paragraph. If nine hundred people were killed in a ferryboat disaster in India, it was worth about two sentences, and so forth.

'Here's a recent one,' the old lady said. I took a wary look. HIT-RUN DRIVER KILLS ALTAR BOY.

'We're getting warmer,' I said. The old lady was trying to be nice. It was just the situation that was starting to look ugly.

'Eight years ago,' she said. I looked. JAPANESE SWIM TEAM NIPS US. That wasn't it.

'Ten years ago,' she piped. It was another story from India. The headline was STORM RIPS CEMETERY – 500 FOUND DEAD.

'We're getting warmer still,' I said. I was about ready to squash this kindly old lady like a bug and cut her into microfilm when she laid another dusty piece of newsprint before me. What was the use? The whole damn place was full of yesterday's fish wrappers anyway. I took an apathetic half glance at the paper on the table. Then my eyes lit up like a Christmas tree in Las Vegas. I jumped up and practically hugged the old lady.

'I need a copy of this,' I said.

Ten minutes later I was leaving the building with a renewed confidence and a large brown folder under my arm when I ran into Bob Miller, the city editor, in the hall.

'You think they'll nail McGovern?' he asked.

'I sure hope not,' I said.

'I sure hope not too,' he said. 'He's selling a hell of a lot of goddamn newspapers.'

## 25

It was after six by the time I got back to Vandam Street and I was hungry and so was the cat. I fed the cat some tuna, and for myself I located an old Italian salami that had fallen into the back of the refrigerator and had been there since about Purim of 1974. Those things will keep forever. Life is short but Italian salamis are long. I ate the son of a bitch with a little leftover shredded wheat that was hanging around and washed it down with some white wine. I wasn't sure what year the wine was but whatever it was, the salami was older. There wasn't much in the house. Had to go shopping one of these days. Right now I couldn't be bothered with food. I was shopping for a maniac.

Unfortunately, he was also shopping for me.

I had a few hours to kill so I thought I'd reestablish commo with Cynthia and Nina, whom I hadn't forgotten about, and try to run down a two-legged arachnid named Barry Campbell. Adrian, I knew, would always be where she was both figuratively and literally. Coke dealers I had known were invariably creatures of narrow habit. They were a lot like cats except that cats had more soul.

Some coke dealers would travel into Harlem at four o'clock in the morning to deliver half a gram and others wouldn't venture across the street because they didn't believe in giving curb service. Whatever their habits and ways were, you could bet they would never dream of changing them to save their lives. Or your life.

So I lit a cigar and dialed Cynthia's number through the smoke. She sounded like hell but I really couldn't blame her. Why did women ever fall in love with guys like McGovern? Why not find some nice slick advertising guy with pleated pants? This was New York, for God's sake. Men were everywhere, and at least some of them weren't homosexual. I wasn't. At least I didn't think so.

'Hi, honey, how're you doing?' I said.

'I'm here,' she said. 'I haven't heard from McGovern.'

'You will,' I said. I was hoping it wouldn't be through the obits or the police blotter, but all I said was 'You will' again very sagely. Maybe she would.

'I just wish this was over,' she said.

'It will be over soon,' I said. 'And I do mean o-v-e-r. I found something in the newspaper morgue today that may be pertinent. I am making headway, believe me.' I didn't know if I believed me but it sounded like she did.

'Don't forget McGovern's a big boy. I'll see you tomorrow.' McGovern wasn't just a big boy. He was also a big nerd. I was just waiting for him to crack like the ceiling plaster underneath a lesbian dance class.

I dialed Nina Kong's number. She wasn't home and pretty soon I wasn't either. I was on my way to meet Ratso at the Ear Inn to hear some kind of iambic pentameter drivel from Peter Myers.

I knew I was getting into deep waters. I didn't reckon though, that it was going to be a bottomless lagoon.

## 26

The evening was crisp and beautiful, a particularly horrible night to have to sit while some pompous lisping self-righteous buffoon bent your ear at the Ear. The moon was up and the cobblestones were beckoning so I took a little walk through the Village. These modern poet-type people were usually so long-winded I doubted if I'd be missing much if I got to the Ear an hour late. If I never went there for the rest of my life I doubted if I'd be missing much.

But Ratso would be there. And of course Pete Myers.

I had just about settled the age-old dilemma of espresso versus cappuccino in favor of cappuccino when the Blue Mill Tavern loomed up in front of me and I walked in and ordered a Jameson. The Blue Mill was a place where a lot of old people usually congregated and the demographics were such that no matter who you were, you always felt young there. McGovern never much favored the place. Said it was the kind of place where Irish bartenders take their families on weekends. Not enough action for McGovern. But Monday night at the Blue Mill was perfect for me. I downed the Jameson and ordered another one with a Prior's dark and went to the telephone to call Nina.

'Hey,' she said, 'you just caught me. We're going into the studio tonight to start on the video. Why not come by some night this week?'

'Okay, I'll do it,' I said. I got the name of the place and the directions. I remembered music when it was still music but I wasn't going to paddle against the wave of the future. Not on one Jameson. 'Maybe tomorrow night,' I said.

'Great,' she said. 'We'd be honored to have you.'

'I'd be honored to have you,' I said and hung up.

I went back to the bar, finished the drinks, ordered another round, and took an old newspaper clipping out of my hunting vest. I put it on the bar in front of me, and when the bartender returned, he put a shot of Jameson on the left of the article and the glass of beer on the right.

'Nice placement job,' I said. I looked over the article again just to be sure I hadn't been dreaming, and it was still the same one I'd gotten from the lady in the newspaper morgue. The story was about four years old. If it had been a Havana cigar, a racehorse, or a French wine, it probably would be coming into its own about now and boding well for all. As it was, it was an old news story that didn't bode especially well for anyone. It was written by a *Daily News* reporter who appeared to have cracked a gay drug ring in the Village.

The reporter, of course, was McGovern. One of those charged was, of course, my old pal Barry Campbell.

Why didn't people ever tell me things before I went chasing after mermaids?

I left the Blue Mill Tavern feeling a lot better for what I'd been thinking and what I'd been drinking. I took a fresh cigar out of my hunting vest and paused by a doorway on Barrow Street to light it. As I rolled the cigar around between my thumb and fingers, always keeping it well above the actual flame, I glanced around me. I was good enough by now to light a cigar in my sleep and probably I would have if it weren't for the fire hazards.

My eyes went to a poster on the wall a little bit above my head. It showed four people in what could only be described as hideously contorted positions. Either they were war victims of some sort or the whirling dervishes were back in town. Underneath that it said WINNIE KATZ'S EXPERIMENTAL DANCE CLASSES FOR WOMEN.

It wasn't something you'd ever want to laugh at out loud, but I did chuckle a bit as I walked off in the general direction of the Ear Inn. 'So that's what they call it,' I said.

## 27

I entered the Ear as surreptitiously as a stray Q-Tip but was captured by Martin, the owner of the place, before I got by the bar. 'Cheers,' he said, as he laid a shot on the bar for me. Martin was a Brit too. Or maybe he was Irish. They all looked the same to me.

I stared into the main room of the Ear where some guy was spouting forth and the ten tables in the place were full of people listening raptly.

'Bit of culture never hurts anything but the cash register,' said Martin.

'You know how I love your poetry nights, Martin,' I said, indicating with my thumb the poet on the stage. 'I'd like to buy that bastard a muzzle for Christmas. How many more are left? They all recite the Yellow Pages, don't they?'

'There's about three or four more who'll be giving readings. Have you ever heard Peter Myers?'

'Yeah,' I said, 'he's terrific. He's the bee's knees.'

It was a quaint place all right, with a giant skylight, pictures of old battleships on the walls, and crayons at the table for customers to draw on the paper tablecloths when they got bored with the poetry readings. I took a few steps into the main room. A figure was slumping semicomatose in a chair at a corner table. Almost all of his body was under the table except for his head and his feet. The prehistoric shoes looked familiar. They'd obviously once belonged to a person who was no longer with us. I couldn't see how the figure was clothed, but I checked the head and it was Ratso's. There were a number of empty bottles on the table. He'd apparently been there since eight o'clock and he did not look pleased.

I walked over and sat down. 'Kind of exciting, isn't it?' I whispered.

'Keep on your toes,' he whispered back.

'Why?' I asked. 'They raise the urinals in this joint?'

The guy standing on the tiny stage never missed a chance to take a simple idea and intellectualize it until it disappeared completely. I didn't know what he was yapping about and I didn't much give a damn. I wished I could get a forklift to get him out of there.

Ratso was sitting up now. 'Keep on your toes,' he whispered, 'because Barry Campbell's sitting over there in the far corner.'

'Good,' I said. 'I'd like to harm that child.' I signaled the waitress and she took our order. Four shots of Jameson and a cup of coffee for Ratso. Had to keep the boy straight.

The drinks arrived about the time Pete Myers hit the stage, which was a good thing because the guy was a driving bore. You couldn't've told that to Barry Campbell though. He was hanging on every word. I'd like to have seen him hanging from a shower rod.

Myers went on interminably and Ratso and I drank. What else could a sane person do? Finally it was over. It was about 10.45. To this day I have no idea what he was reading. The people who weren't brain dead after two and a half hours of poetry recitations applauded politely, and the room broke up into small clusters of people.

'Keep your eye on Campbell,' I told Ratso. 'I'm going to have a word with Myers.'

Myers was talking to an eager young couple. 'Excuse me, Pete, can I have a word with you? It's rather important,' I said. Everybody in this frigging town thought that what they were doing and saying was important so I might as well lie like the rest of them.

'Glad you could get by,' he said. 'How's the Frank Worthington thing going?'

'Well, now that you've asked, maybe you can help me. "Gather ye rosebuds while ye may." Who wrote that?'

I'd already checked it out and it was Robert Herrick, one of the lesser-known British poets, 1591 to 1674. 'Gather ye rosebuds' had been his one big hit apparently.

Myers stroked what there was of his chin for a moment and then offered ponderously: 'I'd have to say John Donne.' Some expert.

'I'd have to say Pete Myers,' I said. I was about half drunk. When you're half drunk, it's hard to tell if you're drunk or sober. I don't really know what I was trying to prove. Maybe nothing. Maybe just get some reaction. Whatever I was trying to do, it didn't work. Myers laughed and made small talk and told me the two of us should stay in touch. By the time I got back to the table Ratso was gone. I looked across the room and so was Barry Campbell.

I looked in the men's room, the ladies' room, and under a few tables, and finally I walked outside hoping to catch a glimpse of someone I knew.

I heard a noise like a car backfiring. I'd heard cars backfiring almost every day of my life but this time I was fresh out of luck. Something sang through my left shoulder and sawed a nice ragged section out of the other side. A swarm of killer bees was buzzing around in my brain as I sank into one of the less populated sidewalks of New York. It was raining blood.

## 28

I came to in the meat wagon. I wasn't sure if I was on the way to the hospital or the morgue, and I didn't give a flying Canadian which as long as I got there in a hurry. The gestapo sirens weren't doing my nerves a lot of good but they weren't as bad as the potholes.

It wouldn't be too unpleasant to be lying on a nice sunny beach right now instead of a meat wagon. But something was always happening to put a crimp in one's vacation plans.

The nurses at St Vincent's were very nice except that one of them looked like the Weasel. Maybe I wasn't seeing too well. It felt like I had a fork sticking in my left iris. Maybe it was The Weasel's sister. Have to make a note to ask him if he had a sister who was a nurse. Better a nurse than a nerd, I thought. My mind was beginning to clear but it was still about as lucid as tripe soup.

Ratso came walking through the fog in a pair of red pants that hurt me. He sat down in the chair next to my bed.

'It'll take more than Barry Campbell's little gang of killer fags to nail you, won't it, pal?' he said.

'Oh, I don't know,' I said. 'I thought they nailed me pretty good this time.'

'Nah, it's only a flesh wound.' Unfortunately, it was my flesh.

'What day is it?'

'It's Tuesday morning.'

'Gotta get out of here.'

'Look, the cops are onto the Campbell thing already. They'll probably be wanting to talk to you. But right now there's a visitor outside that's been waiting to see you. She's been very worried. If it's okay with you I'll get her.' Ratso left the room and a few minutes passed before the door opened again. It was Cynthia.

She sat down and took my hand without saying anything for a while. I had to admit it felt good to have her there. Nina was probably too busy or else she didn't know yet. It didn't matter. Maybe video was Nina's life. Cynthia was a woman. And she was here.

Funny how getting nearly blown away could make you appreciate someone.

'Cynthia,' I said. For a moment I entertained a fleeting thought of jumping her bones but I soon realized what a sick chicken that would make me both physically and spiritually. She looked ravishing. Maybe I was sicker than I thought.

'Are you in great pain?' she asked.

'No. It only hurts when I get excited. Like when I think of how I'm going to rip out McGovern's lungs when I see him.'

'You know, I'm not going to be a guilty woman and say it's all my fault and everything. It's not all my fault. I know. But if McGovern had trusted me more, had believed in me like I believed in him, this wouldn't have happened. He wouldn't have been drinking so much, having nightmares, shouting curses in his sleep. He wouldn't be seeing ghosts in hallways and running from the police. I wouldn't be worn to a frazzle and this would never have happened to you. If he'd only trusted me.'

'Cynthia,' I said, 'did you know that McGovern was the yo-yo champ of the state of Utah when he was only twelve years old?'

She laughed incredulously. 'He wasn't,' she said.

'It's the God's truth. He was. And the bastard's still a yo-yo as far as I'm concerned. First of all, I was minding my own business one afternoon when he called me to come over because there was a stiff in the apartment across the hall. A week later there's two stiffs. And last night I damn near made it a ménage à trois. Now the bastards pulled his patented disappearing act, which he might have gone and done even if the cops weren't looking for him. He will do that, you know.'

'I know,' she said with a wistful smile.

'And he's made the case extremely difficult to make head or tail of even for an experienced veteran sleuth like myself.' I was worn out from talking. I preferred just looking at Cynthia anyway. This time when she hugged me I didn't mind.

I held her for a moment and just at that moment Ratso came back into the room winking at me lasciviously. Cynthia got off the bed, whispered good-bye, and said she'd check on me the next day.

Ratso walked her out the door and when he came back into the room he was smiling. 'I've been waiting for the love interest to come into play. Maybe she'll nurse you through your illness and you two will fall in love.'

'If she's not careful, I may try nursing her first,' I said. 'Help me get out of here, pal, will you?'

'Yeah, I'll help you get out of here. But I'm coming with you and moving in with you for a while. I can sleep on the couch. I just don't trust this whole situation. I'll tell you the truth, Sherlock, your latest case really gives me the heebie-jeebies. So you've got a new roommate until the case is solved.'

He seemed adamant and I was feeling too weak to argue with him.

It was a rare case of a rat joining a sinking ship.

## 29

It was Wednesday afternoon and a light rain was falling on the Village and the town. This was my favorite kind of weather because it reminded me of Vermont or Seattle or some place I'd just visited once and never stayed long enough to learn to hate.

Mick Brennan was futzing around with his camera equipment in my living room and simultaneously overseeing the brewing of some tea in the kitchen. He was a man of many talents.

Ratso and I were having coffee at the kitchen table. He was poring over the documents of the case, i.e., the article on Barry Campbell and Parts 1 to 4 of 'Diary of a Murder Suspect.' I was monitoring the rain and trying to recall what it was I was trying to recall. Whatever it might have been, it remained like a Japanese fishing boat just beyond the territorial waters of my memory and nothing I could do seemed to bring it any closer. I felt fine as long as nobody frogged me in the shoulder.

'You know,' Ratso said as he started knocking down a toasted bagel with nova, cream cheese, onion, and tomato, 'in Part Four here . . .'

'Diary of an Idiot?'

'Yeah, Diary of an Idiot, Part Four, the author really begins to positively crow like a rooster in heat.'

'Sure. It's very self-aggrandizing. First he thinks he's Gandhi writing from a South African prison, and then when he's on the run from the cops, he progresses to sort of a Jack London presence in which he describes a type of freedom that only he can attain and a life-style that only he can appreciate.'

'You do a disservice to Jack London and Gandhi,' said Ratso.

'What are they? Your family's patron saints or something?'

'I knew you weren't going to make a good roommate,' Ratso said, as he located some pickles fresh from the Carnegie Delicatessen.

'Just as long as you don't complain about the room service,' I said. 'Actually, there's not one solid fact in any of McGovern's first four articles that brings us one step closer to solving the killings.'

'Maybe Part Five will be the blockbuster.'

'Yeah. Maybe I'll start riding the subways tomorrow.' I looked out the window at the rain slanting down onto the fire escapes across the street. The Japanese fishing boat was still out there too somewhere, but its outline wasn't coming any more clearly into focus. Why were the Japanese always fishing so close to our fire escapes?

'Two friends of yours here, mate,' said Brennan looking down at Greenwich Street from a far window.

'Impossible,' said Ratso. 'He doesn't have two friends.'

'Actually, I have a great many friends,' I said, 'and they come from all walks of life. If you're a very nice, pleasant person and you always think of others, then if you have a lot of friends, it's practically meaningless. But if you're an eccentric, self-directed sort like I am who voyages through the dark and troubled waters of life and doesn't give a damn about anybody and you still have a lot of friends in spite of all that, that could be seen as a sort of tribute to you.'

Ratso got up and walked across the room to where Brennan was standing. 'Yeah, well, these two friends appear to have just emerged from an unmarked squad car.'

'Get back from the windows. Maybe they'll go away.'

'I think you ought to talk to them,' said Ratso. 'They've certainly grilled Campbell by now, maybe even hauled him in. Obviously you were getting too close to something connected with the case or Campbell wouldn't have been so desperate about taking a potshot at you.'

'My dear Ratso, this case is beginning to smell like the shithouse door on a shrimp boat. Now whether Campbell himself took a shot at me, which I doubt, or whether he hired someone to scare me off, which I think is more likely, neither of those actions fit the peculiar modus operandi of the first two killings. Surely you can see that. Campbell's obviously a bit het up about something and I intend to find out what it is. But it could just be something quite extraneous to the case. What we in the detective business sometimes refer to as a "red herring." '

'Well, you've got a couple of nice seagoing images there anyway,' said Ratso, 'red herrings and shrimp boats.'

'You leave those two cops out there in the rain much longer and they'll be seagoing too,' said Brennan. 'What's the drill, mate? It's your house.'

' "Mate" itself is a nice seagoing salutation,' I said. 'If I can bring calm and equanimity to my two houseguests by throwing a goddamn puppet head out the window, I'll damn sure do it.' With my good arm I raised the window and chucked the parachute device down to Fox and Cooperman below. 'They're not going to be too pleased,' I observed.

'Yeah,' said Brennan. 'What do you want me to do with all this photography equipment? Break it down into its component parts?' I thought about it for a minute or two. It was going to look pretty suspicious having all Brennan's surveillance gear scattered around the place. 'Ever taken group photos?' I asked as Fox and Cooperman pounded on the door of the loft.

Ratso went to the door and let Fox and Cooperman in. They were about as damp as the reception I gave them. 'How you doin', hero?' asked Fox.

'Like the dinosaur said, "I'll survive." But if I find Barry Campbell, I'm going to spray his brains all over Gay Street.'

'Let's not get too trigger-happy, pal,' said Cooperman. 'We talked to Campbell. He's got an alibi for the time you were shot and it checks out fine.'

'Yeah? Where as he? At the Turkish baths?'

'No,' said Cooperman, 'he was at a recording studio on Eighth Street watching them make a rock video. Name of the singer was Nina Kong. You ever heard anything by her?'

My shoulder had started to hurt again. 'Yeah,' I said.

'Everybody smile,' said Brennan, and he snapped our picture.

## 30

I stood Fox and Cooperman to a cup of coffee each and eventually they took their leave. The new wrinkle about Barry Campbell and Nina Kong didn't bother me too much. I didn't have to make the bed, but I might still want to lie in it occasionally.

Meanwhile, it was growing dark outside and I had an appointment to keep at my psychiatrist's. Too bad he wasn't going to be there.

We had a few hours to kill before Rambam arrived, so Ratso and Brennan went out for a drink and I stayed home for a drink. For a change of pace I thought I'd have a shot of Jameson and a cigar to go along with it. I found a Havana cigar I'd bought for eleven dollars several years ago in Vancouver. I was sort of saving it for a celebration, but if you saved anything too long these days you'd wind up in the bone orchard and other people would be doing your celebrating for you.

I lopped off the end of the cigar with my Smith & Wesson knife and carefully singed about an inch of it with a wooden match. Always keeping the cigar well above the flame. Lighting a cigar was like wearing a hat or making love. You either knew how to do it or you didn't. And if you didn't know, you didn't know that you didn't know so it was all right as long as I didn't have to watch you.

Of course, when you paid eleven bucks for a cigar, you expected it to stay all night and bring you a warm washcloth when you were through.

Actually the cigar wasn't bad but it was starting to get kind of brittle. A couple more years and it'd be as brittle as my nerves. I heard Rambam yelling up from the sidewalk so I went over to the window, opened it, and threw down the puppet head. I stood there awhile and watched what was left of the rain. The cool, damp air felt good and cleared some of the cigar smoke out of the place, but it didn't do much to clear up what was bugging me about this whole McGovern business.

I could see that Campbell had a revenge motive for framing McGovern, but he still had no motive for whacking Worthington or Darlene Rigby. And why would Nina Kong lie to me about never knowing Barry Campbell? Did she think I was as trusting and innocent as I looked? And there was something else that was bothering me too. Something deeper and more sinister in its nature. There were several key pieces to this psychological jigsaw that were doing their dead-level best not to fit.

A sudden chill caught me and I closed the window but I still felt the chill.

There was a knock at the door and I went over and opened it. There was Rambam dressed all in black, with a knapsack slung over one shoulder and a big smile on his face.

It was after midnight, and from the way this shrink break-in was being plotted, you'd have thought it was Watergate II. Brennan and Ratso had returned and the big smile on Rambam's face had left.

'Very bad idea,' said Rambam, 'very bad idea. You never told me we were going to take these two meatballs with us. We're talking coded key pads; we're talking motion detectors. I think you're crazy to go with four guys. Why don't we bring the Gay Men's Chorus down there while we're at it?'

'Look,' said Ratso, 'you see what shape Sherlock's in. If he goes down there tonight, I'm going with him.'

'That's very moving,' I said, 'but we're not particularly joined at the hip, you know.'

'That's all right,' said Rambam. 'I've got something for Ratso to do.' He was smiling again, but this time it was a smaller, more malicious smile.

'Yeah, I've got something for you to do, too,' said Ratso.

'Look, fellas,' I said, 'this bickering is unseemly. We've got a job to do – get a copy of this shrink's file on Frank Worthington – and I only hope it's worth the risk we're going to be taking. If I can get a clearer picture of his mind, it'll help me a lot.'

'How about a stiff one for the stiff?' said Brennan cheerfully. I poured the whole house a shot and we all drank one to a dead bisexual we'd never met. A worthy subject for a toast if there ever was one.

'Okay,' said Rambam, 'I'm going on a brief scavenger hunt. I'll be back in about two hours and then it's off to Never-Never Land.'

'Don't let the door bang your ass on the way out,' said Ratso.

When Rambam had left I said to Ratso: 'Look, pal, for your own health, education, and welfare don't upset this guy. He's not doing this for you, he's doing this for me and he's absolutely crucial to the operation.'

'He may be crucial,' said Brennan, 'but I'm indispensable.'

'Do me a favor, will you, Mick?' I said. 'Just for tonight try snapping your shutter and shutting your snapper.' I saw Rambam's point. If Moses had been a committee, the Jews would probably never have gotten out of Egypt. On the other hand, I didn't see any other way around it. So I retired to the bedroom to take a little power nap before the night's entertainment. I nodded off thinking about Dr Bock's pipe and the little leather patches on his elbows and feeling better about the whole thing. That's what happens when you mess around with Marvin Barenblatt.

## 31

I don't know exactly what time it was when Rambam got back, but I did remember who it was I was dreaming about. It was Cynthia. I also remembered what she was wearing and it wasn't much. Just a pair of cute pink house slippers and a little pajama top that didn't go down too far but went a long way toward helping the two of us get a little better acquainted.

When Rambam walked in holding a pair of pink house slippers, I thought I was having some kind of a Peace Corps flashback. Two years in the jungles of Borneo will stay with you for a while.

As it turned out, the slippers weren't for me but for Ratso. Rambam gave them to him, went to the closet, and located a bright purple bathrobe and threw that to Ratso also. 'Put 'em on,' he said, 'you've got a friend waiting for you in the car.' It sounded crazy at the time. I thought Rambam had lost touch with the mother ship. But it was a stroke of genius.

Ratso put on the slippers and the robe and finished what he was doing, which was pouring coffee for all of us.

'You're going to make some lucky guy a pretty gnarly housewife,' I said. Brennan packed his equipment up and we all drank the coffee.

'This is it,' I said. 'Let's go.' It was after two in the morning. No one was on the street. The rain had stopped completely. A few newspapers swirled by in a small gust of wind. There were several parked cars on Vandam, one with a hand-lettered sign in the window that said 'No Radio.' There were about five empty garbage trucks parked in a row, and right in front of them, leading the parade, was Rambam's black Jaguar with what looked to be a little white miniature poodle yapping at us from the front seat. 'He belongs to my aunt,' said Rambam. It was the kind of dog that even a lonely old lady would have to think twice about. My cat could have eaten it for breakfast but she didn't like French cooking. We got in.

Rambam gave Ratso a small walkie-talkie to put in the pocket of the bathrobe. His job was to walk the poodle up and down Charles Street and look like he belonged and to call us if he saw suspicious cop activity. We let Ratso and the dog out at Fourth and Charles. 'His name is Dom Pérignon,' said Rambam.

'Thanks,' said Ratso, 'that'll help a lot.'

We parked the car a little further down the block, and the three of us got out. Rambam looked around a little bit. Then he took out a small tension bar and something else I couldn't see and he was through Bock's Segal lock in under a minute. It might have been faster than that. Time seems amplified when you're standing on the street in the middle of the night watching a guy in pink carpet slippers walking a miniature poodle.

Inside the foyer we heard a soft 'click' and the little red light of a motion detector went on and sent Rambam scrambling. 'Oh, shit,' he said, 'we've got sixty seconds tops.' That meant before the call went through to the security service and from there to the cops. Rambam jimmied the key-pad box off the wall and, with breathtaking speed, took two wires that looked like miniature jumper cables from around his neck and short-circuited the box.

Three minutes later we were inside Bock's office, and Rambam was sizing up the filing cabinets. 'That wasn't bad, was it, mate?' Brennan said to me.

Bock had old-fashioned wooden filing cabinets, and Rambam shoved the bottom drawer down and in with a deft movement and that was all it took. In no time I had Worthington's file out and Brennan was setting up the Minox.

It was fortunate that we'd brought Brennan along because the file was about fifty pages in length and the guy's handwriting looked like it was written by a horseshoe crab that happened to be left-handed.

Mick was working as fast as he could but Rambam was starting to get a little nervous. That made me nervous.

'You got it, Mick?' I asked.

'It's a wrap,' he said.

'Okay, boys,' I said, 'let's call in the dogs and piss on the fire.'

'What was that, mate?' asked Brennan.

'Speed-read my lips, pal,' I said: 'Let's get the hell out of here.'

We left the building, got in the car, and located Ratso and Dom Pérignon on the corner where they'd met a blond with a German shepherd. We dropped Brennan off on Bedford Street at the Monkey's Paw, but I extracted a promise that he'd have the film developed and blown up for me by the following day. Twenty minutes later Ratso was asleep on the couch, the cat was out cold on the rocker, and I was in bed hoping it had all been worthwhile.

I was also hoping that Cynthia would come back again. I had a feeling that she would.

## 32

When I got up Thursday morning it was after eleven and Ratso had gone to work. When he wasn't wearing humorous-looking clothing or running around the Village helping me commit felonies, Ratso went about the high-pressure business of his job as an editor. But the important thing about him now was that he was gone.

I dialed Cynthia's number. Lighting a cigar the correct way while dialing a telephone can pose a problem but I managed.

I wasn't really fickle in my attitude toward women; I just didn't care. I'd loved five or six women in my life but I'd only been in love maybe once. And when the person you love more than anyone else in the world kisses a windshield at 95 mph in her Ferrari, everything else falls into perspective.

'Hello, Cynthia,' I said.

'How are you?' a sleepy voice answered. 'I was going to call you.'

'Well, I called you first. How about joining me for a dim sum this morning in Chinatown?' 'Dim sum' was sort of a Chinese breakfast of many small dishes. The words, so I'd been told by a Chinese girlfriend once, meant 'to touch the heart lightly.' That wasn't too bad a description of the effect Cynthia was having on me.

A half hour later I'd picked Cynthia up on Jane Street and we were in a taxi heading up Houston Street toward Chinatown. Traffic was so bad that the driver skirted Broadway and Mott Street and went all the way to the Bowery before hooking a right toward Canal. He explained it would be faster this way. He would also make a few bucks more on the meter, but it was a beautiful day and I could afford to spend a few more simoleons without winding up washing chopsticks.

It wasn't any faster going down the Bowery. Traffic was tied up like a junkie's arm. So I paid the cabbie and we got out about five blocks from Canal Street, which was where Chinatown formally began. Winos hoping for a tip were washing windshields of the stalled cars. Panhandlers were strung out all along the sidewalk like costume jewelry in a gaudy necklace you wouldn't want your girlfriend to wear to a dogfight.

'This area always bums me out,' I said to Cynthia.

She smiled. If you could make a woman smile, you could probably make her laugh, and if you could make a woman laugh, you could probably . . . and then there was McGovern. I tried to put him out of my mind but it wasn't easy.

I took Cynthia to a dim sum place called the Silver Palace at Bowery and Canal where you take an escalator up one floor and you're suddenly confronted by the sight of half the population of Shanghai gnawing on chicken feet. We were seated at a large round table, which we shared with what looked like an extended Chinese family – babies, kids, old folks – everything but the family dog. That was probably one of the things being served on the dim sum carts. These carts were pushed by Chinese women who circled the room like giant birds, squawking the names of their particular dishes over and over again.

If you saw something you liked such as fish lips or eye of newt, you pointed to it and they gave you the dish. When you were finished, they charged you by the number of dishes on the table. There was good dim sum and there was bad dim sum and you never knew which you'd had until about an hour later when if it was good you felt good and if it was bad you walked around for the rest of the day with a bowling ball in your stomach and a baby squid climbing into your upper intestine.

We ordered several dishes, including a few round objects about the size of golf balls that were filled with shrimp meat; the dim sum lady called them 'shrimp balls.'

'They're from a very large shrimp,' I told Cynthia.

'You know I heard from McGovern,' she said.

'Speaking of a very large shrimp.'

'And he gave me a message to give to you and said he'd call you soon. But I'm supposed to give you the message. I warn you he sounded pretty crazy and so does the message, I'm afraid.' Big surprise.

'Spill it,' I said. I got a good grip on my chopsticks.

'He told me to ask you if you remembered the ghost that you didn't believe he saw.'

'Yeah,' I said, 'I remember it.'

'Well, he said to tell you that he didn't see it again.'

## 33

I took Cynthia Floyd home with me to Vandam when we left the Silver Palace. After nearly getting blown away the other night, I didn't enjoy being alone as much as I used to. Maybe I was getting paranoid, but it was becoming quite obvious to me that there was somebody out there, in addition to Dr Bock and Detectives Cooperman and Fox, who didn't particularly think I hung the moon.

Or maybe someone really did admire me but just had a funny way of expressing himself. I didn't want to find out. But it looked like I was going to have to.

'Wait'll you see the place,' I told Cynthia as we rode up together in the freight elevator.

'I can't wait,' she said. She still had her sense of humor. And I still had most of my shoulder.

Seeing the warehouse-baroque outer facade of 199B Vandam all done in dismal battleship gray with occasional touches of graffiti, then passing through the dingy, dust-laden hallway into the freight elevator with its one exposed light bulb did not lead visitors to expect much. It was always a pleasant surprise when I opened the door to reveal a spacious, comfortable, beautifully appointed loft. It wasn't really beautifully appointed but compared to the freight elevator it could have been the Plaza.

Cynthia was impressed. I told her to look around and make herself at home. 'My loft is your loft,' I said.

I stoked up the espresso maker and checked for messages on the answering machine. As often happens, I'd gotten calls from almost all the wrong people. Creditors, anxious, worried women

I couldn't care less about, acquaintances who were just in town for a few days and I couldn't remember who they were, old dope dealers trying to tempt me back into the fold, and Ratso, whose current residence was my couch so I didn't desperately need to talk to him on the phone.

There was no sense waiting for the call that was going to change my life. It would come all right. But those kinds of calls come about seven minutes too late to make any difference.

The only two calls worth remembering at all were from Brennan and Pete Myers. Brennan's message was something to the effect that he would drop the very explicit photographs of the young boys by my place around three o'clock.

Myers wanted to talk to me about the other night. I wasn't even sure which 'other night' he was referring to. I'd had quite a few of them lately.

Cynthia and I sat down at the kitchen table and I poured us each an espresso. She took out a pack of cigarettes and I bummed one. 'Us Merit smokers gotta stick together,' I told her.

I noticed her eyes for the first time really. They weren't just blue. They were fire-engine blue. They looked intelligent, lost, and worried, with maybe a side order of bored. They also looked plenty frightened.

'Relax, kid,' I said. 'Stay here as long as you like. Maybe together we can shed some light on this unfortunate affair.' Things like this McGovern-Worthington business were always happening to girls like Cynthia Floyd, it seemed. Sordid affairs never did seem to quite get hold of slinkier dames like Nina Kong. Of course, both of them had fared a damn sight better than Darlene Rigby. If you wanted to look at it that way.

Outside the rain was falling again but the sun was still shining. 'The devil's beating his wife,' she said in a small voice.

'Yeah,' I said. 'Or at least he's giving her a hard time. Do you understand what McGovern's message to me might have meant?'

'I haven't understood anything McGovern's said for a long time,' she said. 'Even before anything happened to that man across the hall. I don't understand how anybody could murder two people in such a horrible fashion. I don't understand why someone would want to go and take a shot at you.'

'Hey,' I said, 'there's a jungle out there, Jane.' I took off my jacket.

'Let's have a look at that shoulder,' she said. It was still kind of painful to take my shirt off, so she came over and helped me with it. 'You really ought to have that dressing changed. Here, I'll do it for you.' Regular Nurse Ratched, this girl.

She changed the dressing very efficiently and she stood close to me while she did it. She wasn't at all squeamish. From coroners and lab assistants who'd worked at various stiff hotels, I'd learned that most women, indeed, were not very squeamish when viewing gore and dead bodies. The fainting incidence ran about five to one in favor of men over women. Broads could be tough as nails when they wanted to. They could also be soft as the space between McGovern's ears.

But knowing what they could be didn't tell you what they would be. It didn't even tell you what they should be. If you really thought you understood women, you were probably already a latent hairdresser and you needed to make an appointment with Dr Bock. Unfortunately he was out of town.

'I like your cat,' she said, as she slipped her shoes off.

'My cat speaks very highly of you,' I said. The cat was already in her lap. I wouldn't have minded being there myself.

Looking at the two of them I realized, not for the first time, that women and cats had a lot in common. For one thing, neither of them had a particularly well-developed sense of humor. For another, they both went through life governed only by things that either comforted them or intrigued them. They both liked to be stroked and cuddled and they both could pounce when you least expected it. On the whole, I preferred cats to women because cats seldom if ever used the word 'relationship.'

I went over to my desk and got a cigar and I poured out a few more espressos and I fed the cat a late breakfast and Cynthia and I discussed the case.

She said she hadn't really known Frank Worthington at all except to say hello to or in this case good-bye to. She'd seen both Pete Myers and Barry Campbell coming and going from the building on Jane Street and knew they were friends of Worthington. She'd found Campbell attractive and had even exchanged a few heated words with McGovern about him. She'd never seen Nina Kong or the Rigby girl before.

I probed gently into her relationship with Adrian. I didn't really feel there was that much there but it was hard to tell. For one thing, Cynthia had that look of innocence about her. It wasn't just something she'd been born with, it was an achieved innocence, the kind a prostitute has who turns a trick and gives the money to her boyfriend.

Adrian, on the other hand, worked the opposite side of the spiritual fence. Maybe she wasn't the most jaded person I'd ever met, but she did have degeneracy fairly well staked out. I couldn't see the two of them having much to talk about, but opposites will attract a lot more often than they'll repel. Unless it was a simple case of Adrian's repelling me, which she always did very effectively. A little of her went a long way.

I thought I'd try hitting Cynthia with a broadside. 'How much are you into Adrian in the weasel-dust department?' I asked. Any severely stepped-on cocaine I always referred to as weasel-dust, taking the name of course from the original Weasel at the Monkey's Paw.

Around the Village they said that if John Belushi had only done weasel dust he'd be alive today. And then there were those who said that if Karen Carpenter and Mama Cass had only shared that ham sandwich, they'd both be alive today.

I wondered what it would have taken for Darlene Rigby to be alive today. What would she have to have not seen? To have not heard?

Cynthia was looking down at the cat and I was beginning to wonder if it'd gotten her tongue.

## 34

If Cynthia Floyd was having a bit of a hard time with a drug problem, I could empathize with her under the circumstances. The cops were ready to believe McGovern had croaked two people, and the longer he stayed on the lam, the more they were convinced he was guilty. Cynthia didn't know what to believe, and the more weasel dust she consumed, the more serious the whole affair was going to become. At least in her mind. It was a pretty serious affair even outside of her mind, which was exactly where she was going to be if she kept snorting weasel dust.

You couldn't tell anybody about drugs and booze. I'd been there myself, and every time somebody broke out the hard stuff around me, it was still touch and go. I could very easily be there again if I wasn't damn careful. Of course, it was hard to be too careful when you were dealing in the life-and-death business the way I apparently was now. I guess everybody has to deal with the life-and-death business sooner or later, but there was no point in rushing to the downstairs bedroom.

What I wanted to tell Cynthia but didn't was that you had to decide for yourself about cocaine. You had to hit whatever was the bottom for you before you realized there was nowhere left to fall. The bottom for me had come about five years before on a brittle January morning when I was lugging an ounce of the stuff from one place to another place somewhere on the Upper East Side. It could have been any time but it was probably around nine o'clock in the morning. I didn't have my computer with me. I'd been up for six days and felt like a week.

I'd been standing in some street that should have been a bad dream but it wasn't. I passed by a down-at-the-heel Negro who was hopped up on heroin and talking to himself. I saw a total no-hoper stagger by, smashed completely out of his mind with nothing left to hold on to but the bottle in his hand. 'Another satisfied customer,' I remember thinking.

I was numb. I was ticking like the stopwatch they used on *60 Minutes*. I was so high I was starting to get lonely.

Apparently I'd forgotten just about everything including the fact that my cigar was lit and I'd put it back in my breast pocket. I didn't feel hot or cold because I didn't feel anything. That was about the time I hit the bottom.

The precise moment, I think, was when a small kid came up to me and said, 'Hey, mister, your coat's on fire.' I looked at him and I felt like the oldest living veteran of the War Between the States and at that moment I just didn't give a shit whether or not I ever woke up in Kansas.

I wanted to tell Cynthia this.

But now it was a Thursday afternoon and we were standing in my kitchen on Vandam Street in New York City and we were desperately, make it passionately, clinging to each other. We were still on planet earth but you wouldn't know it.

We kissed each other. It was not a friendly kiss. It was the way you kissed somebody when you knew that in a matter of moments you'd be torn from each other's arms forever and thrown to the fish.

'Don't get too attached,' I said.

With reluctance I took her by the hand and walked down the stairs with her. Someone else in the building was evidently using the freight elevator. I walked her to the corner and as I was putting her in a taxi a blue-eyed ocean rolled across a brown-eyed shoreline.

'Who is this dame?' I asked myself. 'How can we possibly have found ourselves in this situation?' She was, after all, McGovern's girl. McGovern was, after all, one of my best buddies. I didn't exactly have character staked out, but next to her I came off like a spiritual Green Beret. And yet . . .

'Will we see each other?' she asked.

'In our dreams,' I said, and as the cab pulled away I found myself fervently hoping that dreams came true.

## 35

On my way back to the loft I met Mick Brennan. Good. It saved wear and tear on the puppet head. We went up together in the freight elevator, which was now yawning like an open tomb in what passed for the lobby.

He had the goods with him right under his arm and I couldn't wait to get at them.

'I hope you appreciate my staying up half the night processing these bloody bastards,' he said.

'I'd like to see what you got first. Maybe you left your finger over the lens cap or something.'

As I was fooling around with the lock on my door, I could hear the phones ringing inside the loft. By the time I got to them, I felt like I'd just done forty squat thrusts in the parking lot.

'This is the Shadow,' a familiar voice said. It was McGovern. 3.17 p.m.

'Go ahead, Shadow, I read you,' I panted. I looked around for another cigar to help me get my wind back. 'Make some tea and some crumpets or something, will you, Mick?' I shouted.

'Righty-ho.'

'Meet you tonight late. Place where Charlie Parker and Edith Piaf used to hang out. Down the street from where I urinated on the lady's leg. Okay?'

'See you there, pal. Are you all right?' I asked.

'Does a chicken have lips?' He hung up.

I knew the place he was referring to. It was a seedy interracial jazz bar down the way from the Monkey's Paw. It made the Paw look chic.

I joined Brennan for a spot of tea. He took out the prints he'd made of Bock's file on Frank Worthington and we looked them over. The physical clarity was remarkable. What clues I might find in a two-and-a-half-year-old shrink report that might pertain to a two-week-old croaking, I wasn't sure.

'Got to be going, mate,' said Brennan. 'The prints and the processing are all on the house, by the way.'

'Well, at least the price is right,' I said. 'Thanks, Mick.' I closed and locked the door behind him as he left. Couldn't be too careful these days. Then I got busy on the blower. First I called my friend Boris, the Russian karate master.

'Boris,' I said, 'can you help us with a job tonight? It could get rough. We may have to put on our lobster bibs.'

'I don't understand,' said Boris, in a deep, thick, and very dangerous accent.

'You will. I'm going to see a guy named Barry Campbell tonight. The last two times I saw him I needed a hospital immediately afterward. Tonight I want to find out what he knows and maybe pay him back if necessary.'

'Good,' said Boris. 'I will choke him.'

'Yeah, but you'll have to be careful. He's got the entire Polish army working for him, and I don't want anybody to end up in the croakee's condominium.'

'I don't understand,' said Boris.

'You will,' I said. I doubted if he would. I didn't understand either. I set the time for ten o'clock at my place and rang off.

I puffed on the cigar and watched as my digital-computer alarm hit 3.47 p.m. Actually the whole situation was alarming but nowhere near as alarming as it was soon going to be.

In a dusty cabinet beneath the sink, I found a shot glass made from an old bull's horn and into it I poured a healthy slug from a new bottle of Jameson. Something old and something new. The something borrowed would have to be my couch, which was still loaded down with Ratso's crap even when Ratso himself wasn't parking his torpedolike body there. And the something blue was my shoulder, which was, to quote Amory Blaine in *This Side of Paradise*, 'blue as the sky, gentlemen.'

Everything was running about par for the course.

I took the shot glass, the bottle, the cigar, and the shrink's report over to my desk, upon which the cat was already putting down roots. I started going over the report. The first thing I noticed was that Frank Worthington's date of birth was in mid-February. Whether he was an Aquarius or a Pisces I wasn't sure, but something fishy was going on here that I should have been alert to before now.

I checked back on the calendar and found the day and the date Worthington had gotten croaked. It was his birthday. Many happy returns, pal.

There was plenty of sickological drivel in the file all right. Dr Bock had seen to that. Worthington was having some problems with his sexual identity, some problems with his interpersonal relationships, and some problems with just about everything else. So what else was new?

I was in the act of pouring another tot of Jameson into the bullhorn when I tripped and fell over a twenty-dollar word in one of Dr Bock's nagging little footnotes. It read: 'The patient at times appears to be living in irrational fear of his doppelgänger.' I called Ratso.

'*National Lampoon*,' the secretary said.

'Yeah. Ratso, please.'

'Just a moment, please.'

'Editorial department.'

'Yeah, Ratso, please.'

'Just a moment, please. May I tell him who's calling?' By all means.

'Yeah. This is Dr Felch calling.'

'One moment, please, Dr Felch.' A little more time elapsed. Someone was probably going into Ratso's office to shake him awake. In another moment he came on the line, businesslike and brusque as he always was when he was in the office.

'Yeah, Felch. What can I do for you?'

'Well, I've come across a rather large kraut word in this shrink's report.'

'What is it?'

'*Doppelgänger*. "The patient at times appears to be living in irrational fear of his doppelgänger." '

'It means he's afraid of his double,' said Ratso.

'Is that all?' I said.

I must have dozed off. My shoulder had been throbbing and I'd been feeling a recurrent chill down my spine but the Jameson had apparently kicked in. I was having a nightmare about doppelgängers and the cat was sitting on the shrink's report right in front of me and about equidistant between the two phones on the desk when they rang. The cat went up like a rocket at 6.17 p.m. and went down like an oil well about five seconds later.

The phones ringing scared the hell out of me, too. But they didn't scare me half as much as what I heard next.

My answering machine was rolling to screen my calls and I got the message down on tape so it wasn't just a part of the nightmare

I was having. It was a nightmare, though, just the same. Except that this one wasn't a dream.

It was an unfamiliar, disembodied, pay-phoney sort of voice, and it didn't sound particularly earthbound.

'This is Frank Worthington,' it said.

## 36

I had about half an hour before Ratso got home to my couch from work so I downshifted from Jameson to coffee, phased the cat gently out of the rocking chair, and tried to take stock of the situation as it was at 6.25 p.m. Thursday night, the chilling, rattling caboose of a frozen February in this year of our landlord 1985.

I had two stiffs, one doppelgänger, one dangerous fruitcake to grill, one fugitive friend to meet. If it had been a pokerhand I would have passed.

If you looked at life in pokerhands, another hand might have been the four suspects – Campbell, Myers, Nina, Adrian – and five would be McGovern if you wanted to count him. One of these cards was quite a joker all right, and I was determined to weed that joker out even if I had to borrow Old McDonald's threshing machine to do it.

I got up and played the phone machine message a few more times. 'This is Frank Worthington . . .' 'This is Frank Worthington . . .' I'd only met him once and that was as a stiff on the floor, but now I was starting to understand his mind, his problems, his dreams, and I also had what purported to be his own voice on my answering machine.

It also crossed my increasingly cluttered desk that if Worthington had been a part-time actor, there might exist a recording of his voice. Maybe a television commercial like, 'Honey, this frozen quiche is delicious!' or 'Honey, these plates really sparkle!' or in Worthington's own particular case, 'Honey, I'm going out bowling with the boys tonight.'

If something like this existed, it could easily be matched with the tape I had to determine my message's authenticity. I was thinking over the possibilities when I remembered I hadn't called Pete Myers back yet. So I did.

'I've identified your poet,' he said.

'What the hell are you talking about?'

' "Gather ye rosebuds while ye may," my friend. It was Robert Herrick, a British romantic poet who wrote in the sixteenth century.'

'Seventeenth,' I said.

'Well, sixteenth and seventeenth, I'd say.'

'He must have been a goddamn prodigy then. He was only about eight and a half years old when the sixteenth century burned its last few witches and ground to a close.'

'Touché,' said Myers. I liked people who said 'touché' about as much as I liked people who said 'ciao.' I didn't even like Italians who said 'ciao,' though if they didn't say it, I could see how they'd probably have a pretty rough time trying to leave a room.

'Look, Myers, did Frank Worthington ever do any voice-overs or television commercials or anything like that, to your knowledge?' I was taking a little chance here that Myers could himself be the one behind my crank call, but that's what life was all about, wasn't it? Taking chances. It was also, of course, what death was all about.

'He did. Yes, he did. When I was . . . uh . . . seeing him, he was with some advertising agency. I think it was called Umbrella, Incorporated, or something like that.'

'Thanks,' I said. 'You want to fall by here sometime tomorrow afternoon?'

'Sure. How about threeish? We can discuss Robert Herrick's development as a poet.'

'Fine. I'll be here. One-ninety-nine-B Vandam. Look up to the fourth floor and holler.' At least Myers was a good sport. I wondered if he was a good shot.

As it turned out, for reasons quite beyond my control, no one but the cat would be here tomorrow afternoon at three o'clock. And the cat knew enough never to let strangers into the apartment.

I was just ciao-ing off with Myers when Ratso walked in.

'Somebody left a message on the machine for you, Ratso,' I said and I played him the tape. 'This is Frank Worthington . . .'

'Jesus,' he said. 'What is that? Somebody's idea of a sick prank?'

'I prefer to think of it as the hand of Satan moving in the world,' I said.

'Looks like somebody out there's sure trying to jerk our chain, doesn't it?'

'Yes, yes, it does, my dear Ratso,' I said. 'It's certainly beginning to appear as if there's a doppelgänger in the woodpile.'

## 37

At ten o'clock sharp a voice louder than a garbage truck shattered the peace of Vandam Street and I hastened to the kitchen window to fling forth the puppet head into the February night. Boris was nothing if he wasn't punctual. Well, actually he was something. He was deadly.

'Ratso,' I said, 'why don't you turn that crap off and get ready to go.' Moving in with me had meant that Ratso had had to make the extreme sacrifice – leave his cable TV and his beloved Ranger games and make do with my small, shabby, dusty black-and-white set that required a screwdriver to turn it on or off or to adjust the volume because the knob had been lost through the carelessness of one of the previous owners. I did supply the screwdriver, but Ratso was still not very happy having to watch *So This is New Jersey* and *Meet the Black Mayors*.

'Great stuff,' he said as he turned off the set with a screwdriver and a good deal of disgust.

'Programming isn't what it used to be,' I said.

Boris was pounding on the door. I walked over and let him in. He had a bottle of vodka, a large loaf of Russian rye bread, and about five pounds of caviar on him, all of which he deposited onto the kitchen table.

'Good,' I said, 'if we get back alive tonight, we'll have a little midnight snack.'

I picked up my Smith & Wesson knife and started to slip it into the old hunting vest but Boris stopped me with a rather decisive and unpleasant gesture. 'Do not take it. You will not need it,' he said.

'You're sure?' I asked.

'I promise,' he said and as he rolled his *r* in *promise*, I rolled my eyes at Ratso. It looked like a fun-filled evening ahead.

The three of us drank a little vodka toast to warm our spirits and then I left the cat in charge and locked the door. On the way down the stairs, Boris said to us, 'You have never seen Boris in action?'

'No,' said Ratso, 'but we've heard stories.'

'Tonight you will see,' said Boris, 'that the stories about Boris are true.' I was sure they were. Boris, blindfolded, putting out lighted matches with a bullwhip. Boris unarmed and single-handedly demolishing a twelve-member street gang in Brooklyn. Boris teaching karate to the school for the blind in Russia. Boris teaching secret North Vietnamese techniques to the NYPD SWAT team. No doubt about it, the boy was good. Also, I admired people who always spoke of themselves in the third person.

We piled into Boris's beat-up little car. 'The heater doesn't work,' he said with some irritation, 'thanks to Rambam.'

'Rambam really gets around,' I said.

'Where to, Sherlock?' asked Ratso.

'Tenth Street and Waverly,' I answered. I'd done a little personal surveillance on Campbell and I knew his movements like the back of my shoulder. His movements weren't real complex. When he wasn't dressed up like a mermaid shimmering across the waves and flapping his tail at the denizens of the Blue Canary, he was running a fairly steady tattoo back and forth from his home on West Tenth Street to the gay bar on the corner called Julius's. Some life.

If you plumbed deeply enough into the triple-decker sandwich of the mind until you reached that Land of Oz, the subconscious, you'd find that every homosexual was a heterosexual and that every heterosexual was a homosexual. You'd probably also find that neither group was too fond of Sigmund Freud.

Boris parked the car on Waverly in the middle of the block.

Julius's bar was in plain sight on the corner. The place was practically a Village landmark. It had been there since Adam and Steve.

I told Boris and Ratso to wait in the car and if I wasn't out of there in twenty minutes to send in the Marines. What a scene that would have been.

I walked into the place tough and assured, feeling kind of like the Marlboro Man. Fortunately nobody asked me to light their Lucky. There were about a hundred guys in the place already, laughing, drinking, and making whatever passed for gay cocktail chatter. Sounded like somebody was masturbating tiny little baby chipmunks.

'Turkey on the rocks,' I told the bartender. I wanted a suitably masculine drink. Not that there was anything wrong with Jameson. Hell, no.

I casually glanced around through the cigarette smoke and over the bobbing heads of Julius's clientele. I was a man among men all right. Not a dame in sight unless you wanted to count the middle-aged queen at the end of the bar and I didn't. Barry Campbell was not there.

I fished through the crap in my pocket and came up with a scrap of paper with his number on it. I walked over to the pay phone and plunked in a quarter. I let the phone ring about nine times. No Campbell. I checked information for the number of the Blue Canary, called there, and learned Campbell wasn't working tonight.

I hung up and walked back to the bar and ordered another Turkey on the rocks and waited.

About seven minutes later Campbell came into the bar. There were the usual greetings: 'Hey, Barry,' 'Hello, sweetie,' 'Hi, big fella.' He was quite a popular character, well liked by his peers. He walked over to the bar and the bartender said: 'Will it be the usual, Barry?' I was dying to know what the usual was. Probably a pink lady. A brandy Alexander.

The bartender poured him a Turkey on the rocks.

'So much for appearances,' I said.

Campbell looked over at me, registered shock, started to bolt, apparently thought better of it, stayed put, and took a slug of Wild Turkey.

'What the hell are you doing here?' he asked belligerently.

'Thought I'd have a drink with the boys,' I said. 'Join me at a table?'

Campbell looked furtively around the bar. 'All right,' he said. 'Let's get this over with.'

We threaded our way through the fashion plates, the truck drivers who weren't truck drivers, and the longshoremen who'd never seen a ship up close unless it was a ferry.

There were even a few guys who looked like insurance salesmen or accountants. I didn't know if they were the real thing or not, but I wasn't going to find out. We found an empty table in the back and sat down.

'Campbell,' I said, 'we're going to pass for the moment on what happened to my mind and my left shoulder last Monday night. We'll take that up later, I assure you. But right now I want you to cast your mind back nearly two weeks ago to a Friday afternoon when you sent Frank Worthington some flowers. How many flowers did you send him and why?' I took out a cigar and started to fool around with it preparatory to lighting. Before I could strike a match, he blurted the answer.

'A dozen roses,' he sneered. 'It was his friggin' birthday, that's why. Anything on the books against that?'

'Nothing on the books,' I said. In my book Campbell was one under-the-weather chicken.

'What're you drinking Wild Turkey for?' I asked. 'I thought you were big on Bloody Marys.'

'I like a little variety,' he said.

'Yeah,' I said, looking around the place, 'I can see that.'

'What else is on your mind, big guy?' said Campbell.

'Where were you that Friday, Campbell? Did you attend a little birthday party for Worthington?'

'Yeah. I was over there.'

'Bring the roses with you?'

'No. I had them sent in the morning. I stopped by about two o'clock to party a little with Frank.'

'Remind me not to invite you to my next affair,' I said. 'Did anybody else stop by while you were there? How long did you stay?'

'I stayed about an hour. Pete Myers was just arriving when I left. He was carrying the banana bread. He's a great cook. Quite a fine poet, too.'

'Sounds like a real all-around guy,' I said. 'You didn't notice if he was wearing any lipstick, did you? We found some on one of the glasses.'

'That's very funny,' said Campbell. 'No, he wasn't. Is that all now?' Campbell stood up to leave. He was starting to look a little nervous.

'What's the matter, Campbell? You're looking a little green around the gills if you'll pardon the expression.'

'I don't have to take this shit from you. I don't have to take this shit from anybody,' he said and he strode out of the place like an angry little rooster. My twenty minutes were up anyway.

'Whatever did you say to Barry?' somebody in the crowd asked me as I headed for the door.

'I told him his pants were on fire,' I said without turning around or slowing my pace. I wanted to get out of there in at least the same lousy shape I was in when I had first entered the joint.

It didn't look like anybody was following me. Didn't really hurt my ego though. I stood out on the sidewalk for a moment. I looked around but Barry Campbell was as gone as a goose in winter. It was a good thing he was gone, too. He was starting to get on what was left of my nerves.

I took out a cigar and was going to light it when a beautiful young woman walked by. I put out the match and watched her as she moved farther down the sidewalk. A rather willowy young man was leaning against the doorway of the club smoking a cigarette and gazing desultorily at the girl. He killed his cigarette. I lit my cigar.

'Almost makes you wish you were a lesbian, doesn't it, pal?' I said.

## 38

I looked up and down the street. It was as peaceful as any little village you ever saw. The clock in the old church tower on Tenth Street said eleven-thirty. If it could've talked it would've said a hell of a lot more.

The sleepy little village was just waking up. It was what they call a 'late town.' Many of the trendier clubs hadn't even opened yet. Pretty soon all hell would break loose, I figured. Actually, it broke loose a little sooner than that.

I walked back up the block to where Boris and Ratso were shivering in the little car. 'It's about time, Senator,' said Ratso. 'I was beginning to think you were turning over a new life-style.' I got into the car. It was colder than a hockey puck in there and it was almost as small.

As Boris started her up, a big new Lincoln pulled up on the street in front of us to double-park. It appeared to have a full complement of adult white males inside as far as I could see, which evidently wasn't far enough.

Boris backed his little car up as far as he could and cut the wheel. He probably would've tried to honk a few times except that his horn worked about as well as his heater. The big Lincoln inched forward a bit as if to let us out, but then it swiftly glided back again in one smooth motion like a graceful urban shark. The situation didn't look too promising. I didn't really want to get my last supper served to me on New Jersey plates.

'Too bad we don't have the other kind of heater either,' said Ratso.

'What do you mean?' asked Boris.

'Later,' Ratso said distractedly from the back seat, 'later.'

'That's being a bit presumptuous, isn't it? You're assuming there'll be a later.' Being right there next to Boris made me more cocky than usual. It was clearly going to be a tension convention of some sort, and I knew from recent experience that I wasn't bulletproof, but I still felt pretty confident about handling the situation.

The guys in the car, what I could see of them, looked like well-dressed, fairly bored professionals, but they were large specimens and there was something about their demeanor that was as serious as cancer.

I couldn't really be sure that these birds had any connections with Barry Campbell, but the last two times I'd seen the guy something unpleasant had happened to me and this time it looked like he was going for the hat trick. These goons obviously wanted to take our parking place but the trouble was that they seemed to want us to still be in it.

Ratso made a move to open the door. 'Stay in the car,' I said. That's usually good advice in these situations. The only better advice would have been to stay in bed that morning. He wasn't going anywhere anyway. It was a two-door car. He was a trapped rat if these guys got out. All three of us were. But one of us was Boris.

This thought cheered me ever so slightly, as if I'd just snorted about a half gram of courage heavily cut with stupidity. I hollered. 'Hey, move it!' but the guys in the Lincoln didn't even turn their heads. They looked as dangerous and amoral as store mannequins but not quite as sensitive.

Something had to break and I knew that whatever it was, it wasn't going to be my heart, so I rolled down my window and stuck my head out of the little car and yelled at the driver: 'Hey, pal! You want to move your father's mortgage?'

It worked like a signal from the Old North Church. Four haircuts in aluminum suits piled out of the Lincoln and came right at us.

'Holy shit,' said Ratso.

'Tell me about it,' I said as I frantically tried to roll up the window.

Moments like these you'd be surprised how much can go through your mind. Not that your whole life flashes before your eyes or anything like that. Nothing that tedious. But you do have time for a few little irrelevancies here and there. I thought about guys like Barry Campbell. There are guys that look gay and there are guys that don't look gay and there are guys that you can't tell if they're gay or not when they're walking down the street until they turn and go into the Caffé Sha Sha. Campbell was one of this last group of guys. But once you knew he was gay, it became pretty obvious and you usually convinced yourself that you'd known all along.

I thought in a fraction of a second about Nina Kong. She didn't seem like the type to turn into a lying welcher. Maybe all women had the potential. Maybe all people had the potential. Horrifying thought. Why would Nina lie to me and tell me she didn't know Barry Campbell and then I get some lead lodged in my shoulder blade and his alibi is that he's watching her make her video? Maybe he was just a fast worker. But I remembered the knowing way he winked at her that night at Chumley's. It seemed like another world. Another lifetime. Guess I wouldn't be getting down to Texas to see the folks this summer. I might get to see some interesting coral formations or some exotic fish or whatever you see at the bottom of the Hudson River when you're wearing cement wheels or a nice Italian suit of scrap iron. Come to think of it, they probably didn't have coral formations or exotic fish in the Hudson River. But they might have mermaids swimming in and out of sunken Japanese fishing boats.

And Cynthia. Hard to believe that a beautiful blonde could have wormed her way into my gypsy heart. Probably should have hosed her when I had the chance. Would have if it hadn't been for McGovern. McGovern. McGovern was the root of all evil . . .

I was still cursing McGovern when the door on my side of the car was torn open like a can of sardines. There was a man out there standing on the sidewalk and I came about eye level to his kneecaps. If he was wearing a head I couldn't see it.

Whatever he had on above his neck, there wasn't time for him to get complacent about it. I heard a number of repeated explosions somewhere on the roof of Boris's car, and when I looked around for Boris, he wasn't there but at least two other sets of kneecaps were. Later I heard from a homosexual bystander who shall remain anonymous probably for his whole life that Boris was on top of the car pounding the head that belonged to my guy's set of kneecaps into the metal roof while the other guys were running around furiously grabbing for Boris. From my vantage point all I could see really clearly was a number of teeth skittering down over the windshield and bouncing a couple of times on the hood. It looked like somebody had sabotaged a Chiclet factory.

I levelled a solid kick between one of the sets of kneecaps and a little above, and apparently I connected because I heard a howling noise a few stories up. I saw daylight and I scuttled out and backward on the driver's side like a frightened crab ready to pinch the world. I looked over the top of the car and saw Boris field-stripping a guy on the sidewalk. I turned around just in time to catch a freight train right between the eyes and I had to take the mandatory eight count. Several shots rang out across the barroom floor and I saw a face that looked a lot like Ratso's receding rapidly in the window of a spaceship. I could still see, I just couldn't quite pick myself up off the canvas or the sawdust or the ocean bed or wherever the hell I was currently deep-sixed.

Boris was doing some sort of sinister ballet moves. His partner was a big blond fellow, but by the time Boris had tapped the guy behind his left ear with a few fingers and rammed his nose about halfway through his brain, the guy was a redhead and he was lying next to me on the street. The reason I say left ear was because that was the only ear the guy had left.

Ratso was now out of the car and helping me up and either the big black shark was receding or else my hairline was.

## 39

As we drove away, Boris was laughing deeply and heartily and ranting against peasants, soldiers, fools, and cossacks. Ratso was laughing too, but a little nervously, I thought. I would've been laughing but I tried it a few times and it made my head hurt, so I just smiled serenely like a Moonie on LSD. It felt good to be alive when very recently you didn't think you would be.

'Hey, Ratso,' I said, 'you really got out there into the thick of things.'

'I couldn't get the goddamn seat to go forward.'

'If the seat had not been broken, you would be dead,' said Boris gravely.

'We don't know that,' I said.

'Yes, we do,' said Boris. 'You were very lucky.'

I didn't know it then but that was about as lucky as I was going to get that Thursday night. Lady Luck had other commitments apparently. Maybe she was in Atlantic City or Monte Carlo. Or maybe it was just something I had said to her.

It was midnight. It had almost been a damn sight later than that.

Boris drove around the Village a bit and parked the little car next to a handy hydrant on Fourth Street. We walked over to the Monkey's Paw for a beverage or two and I noticed The Weasel was tying up the pay phone with one of his business calls and I'd forgotten to bring my crowbar.

I made a mental note to speak to Cynthia the following morning. I didn't need anybody else to know that I was in contact with McGovern, so I didn't tell Ratso or Boris both for my protection and for theirs. And I wanted to warn Cynthia about talking to Adrian. Adrian was on a search and self-destruct mission in life and she didn't give a damn who she took with her. And Cynthia was just the kind that could get taken.

It was easier to spill your heart to a coke dealer than it was to a bartender or a shrink or the man at the Greyhound station. If Cynthia needed a confidant, she could talk to me. Discretion was my middle name.

After a few shots I was feeling better than I had in years. It always seemed that way for about an hour. I even started listening to Ratso's account to Tommy the bartender of the evening's little fracas. It didn't sound like the same evening.

I told Boris to collect Ratso in a little while and I'd meet them around two-thirty in the morning at my place for vodka and caviar. If you've got to have vodka and caviar, two-thirty in the morning is as good a time as any. And I didn't want to hurt Boris's feelings.

Boris was smiling a big, satisfied smile as I ankled it out of the joint. As I slipped out the front door I could hear Ratso telling the whole left side of the bar: 'So I says to the guy, "You're not gonna push me around like a little red apple . . ." '

It was raining in Sheridan Square, which made it look all the better because it cut the visibility. In the rain it looked lonely and crowded at the same time, and all the people looked just like people in the rain. They say the rain washes everybody clean, but the rain had its work cut out for it in Sheridan Square.

I was just enjoying the negative ions out on the sidewalk when I turned to see a pair of beady, nervous little orbs knifing their way into my back. It was a face that managed to look frightened, threatening, desperate, and predatory at the same time, as well as reflecting several other sicker emotions. It wasn't a bad appetite depressant but just about everything else about the face was bad. And the voice behind the face was worse.

'You're a liar. You're a scumbag!' it said.

'Mr Scumbag to you, pal,' I said. It was The Weasel. He hadn't wanted to create a disturbance in his place of business, so he'd followed me out there in the rain. Mean little bastard would have probably followed me into hell just so he wouldn't make waves in the marketplace.

'What's distressing you, Max?' I asked. 'Haven't you gotten enough money together yet to go to Rome and paint your masterpiece?'

A mask of cold hate fell across his mean little countenance and it gave me a turn, but I figured I'd finish the thought. Might as well, he hadn't shot me yet.

'After all, you have had a broad range of experience. Not everybody's spent ten years in the men's room of the Paw and lived to tell about it. And I think you've got a certain artistic flair . . .'

'Shut up!' he screamed like an emotionally disturbed little girl. What a tragedy for me to escape four haircuts in aluminum suits only to be drilled by a weasel.

'You-set-me-up,' he stammered. 'The cops are onto me. Those names I gave you. They want my blood . . .'

'What's in a name, Weasel?' He was already so convulsed it was hard to tell if he even heard me.

'We're not friends. I don't like you,' he shouted. Hearing a middle-aged man talk this way was frightening. I turned and walked toward Village Cigars, quite aware that the Village Cigar sign might well be the last thing I was ever going to see on the short little merry-go-round ride some of us call life.

I took about twelve steps and then I turned to look. There was no Weasel. There was only the rain where The Weasel had been. He'd either disappeared like some demon in a dismal night or he'd gone back into the men's room from whence he'd sprung. I was surprised to find my hands were trembling and the flesh was creeping a little on the back of my neck. 'Nothing like a good cigar on a rainy night,' I thought, and I walked briskly across a rain-swept Seventh Avenue in the direction of the old Village Cigar sign.

There was a guy on the corner trying to collect money to fight AIDS. He shouted: 'Money for AIDS – not for war!' Over his head hung a rain-drenched banner that said: IF THE WORLD BLOWS UP YOU CAN'T BE GAY.

That was certainly true.

## 40

I was smoking an expensive rope from the Dominican Republic when I walked down the three steps into the joint called the High Five. It was pushing one o'clock. I bought a shot of snake piss and I looked around through the smoke. McGovern was there all right, about twice as big as God, sitting at a little table in the corner. I walked over and sat down across from him.

'Hey, pal,' I said.

'Hey, pal,' he said.

'While we're doing a little sober time here together in such intimate surroundings, you'd better spill your little ghost story first.'

'You know Edith Piaf and Charlie Parker probably sat at this same little table.'

'Yeah,' I said, 'they must've been quite an item.' I was running fresh out of charm. 'Spit it,' I said.

'You know Cynthia once told me the kind of man she loved was the kind that could never attend a black-tie dinner.'

'Some broads today still have a little class,' I said. 'Cynthia's one.' Cynthia was one all right and look where it'd gotten her. She was as miserable as Edith Piaf or Billie Holiday. Sensitivity, character, intelligence: These were little hurdles you had to overcome if you wanted to get anyplace in life. Now take The Weasel, for instance . . .

'Same ghost,' said McGovern. 'Following me. It never says a word, but when I turn around sometimes it's there. Pretty spooky, I'll tell you.'

'McGovern, do you know how silly it sounds to hear this from a grown man?'

'I can't help it. Drunk or sober I still keep seeing the damn thing. I'm snapping my wig. The cops are after me. Maybe I'll just turn myself in.'

'Or you could try pissing up a rope, pal,' I said. I looked in his eyes and immediately felt bad for saying it.

'Jesus Christ, McGovern,' I said. 'Give me till Monday. Give me three more days to solve this thing. We'll turn the goddamn Village upside down and shake it. If I haven't caught the killer by Monday, do what you feel you have to.' This whole thing was getting hairier than the guy in ZZ Top.

'Deal?' I asked.

'Deal,' said McGovern. He looked as shaky as I felt.

'Better stagger our departures,' I said. 'You go first. If there's a ghost waiting out there, there's no point in him scaring the hell out of both of us.'

'Okay,' said McGovern as he got up to leave. 'It's just a good thing that I'm so tall.'

'Why is that, McGovern?' I asked.

'Because I think I'm in some deep shit,' he said.

The cab let me off on Vandam Street between two garbage trucks. It was two-thirty in the morning, the time a Chinaman goes to his dentist. I looked up from the street and saw that the lights were all burning on the fourth floor. Some bastard had taken the freight elevator again, so I legged it up the stairs and got my key out to unlock the door. Even then I knew that something was wrong. When I opened the door I knew what it was.

Detective Sergeants Fox and Cooperman were standing in my kitchen. Ratso and Boris were at the kitchen table. It didn't look like they'd made much of a dent in the vodka or the caviar. The cat was nowhere to be seen.

'Don't bother taking off your hat,' said Cooperman, 'because you ain't stayin'.'

'Is there a problem, gentlemen?' I asked.

'Yes,' said Fox, 'there is a little problem. Somebody whacked Barry Campbell tonight. Nice professional little job. Two slugs in the back of the head. Body was found in the gutter on Waverly about a block and a half from Gay Street.'

'Remember Gay Street?' asked Cooperman.

'Should I?' I asked. I walked over to the table and picked up the bottle of vodka and put a lip-lock on it. It burned its way down my throat and it felt like Napoleon's whole army was down there retreating in front of it.

'Well,' said Cooperman, 'let me refresh your memory for you. A few days ago you stood in this same room and swore to me and my colleague here that when you found Campbell you'd spray his brains all over Gay Street. Now here we are a week later and we get this report and we go out and who do we find croaked and hugging the gutter? Campbell. Where do we find him? A block and a half off Gay Street. And they were short blocks. Now that's close enough for cop instinct.'

'When I said that, I'd just gotten winged by one of Campbell's goons. I was angry. It was just a figure of speech.'

'Yeah,' said Fox, 'well, you figure a speech out on the way to the precinct. We're taking you in for questioning, pal. Let's move it.'

I caught a brief glimpse of the cat hiding under the sofa and peering out nervously at me as I was escorted through the door.

Cats were pretty smart.

## 41

'Western Union prefers not to transmit that type of message, sir.'

'What the hell. Well, send the first one anyway. Thank you.' I cradled the blower and picked it up again. It was now more than twelve hours later and I had been to hell and back and I hadn't seen Audie Murphy anywhere. Wolf Nachman had finally gotten me out of a hotbox between Fox and Cooperman that had provided an enormous amount of heat and damn little light. I was now engaged in a flurry of activity to try to pull together what few frazzled threads I could find in this mess and weave them into enough of a straitjacket to keep McGovern from turning himself in to the cops on Monday. If McGovern did that, I felt, it would be tantamount to an admission of guilt on his part.

It was 3.47 p.m. on a cold, brisk Friday afternoon, the last Friday in February. I lit a handsome-looking new cigar and took a slurp of hot black coffee. The cat was sitting under her private heat lamp on my desk and watching me as I dialed the number of the ad agency Frank Worthington had once done some commercials for, Umbrella, Inc.

'Umbrella. May I help you?' came the no-nonsense secretary's voice.

'Yeah,' I said. 'Let me speak to Bill Johnson.' Ratso had run down the name for me. The guy was head honcho at the ad agency.

'Who's calling, please?' I didn't like this secretary already. I told her my name.

'What is the call in regard to, sir?'

'Look, all I can tell you is that the matter is very urgent and may possibly involve a life-or-death situation. Now will you find Mr Johnson for me?'

'But what is the call in regard to, sir?' Poor woman, she was running out of patience with me.

'Don't dreidel me, lady. It's about the umbrella he's going to need to keep the crap off his head that's going to come down on him if I don't get to talk to him now . . . Tell him it concerns

Frank Worthington,' I said as a kind of an afterthought, but apparently those were the magic words.

'Just a minute, sir,' she said rather curtly. I waited a little more. Peter Myers was due over any minute, and tonight I intended to dissect Nina Kong like a laboratory frog. The cops were of the opinion that either McGovern, myself, or the mob had croaked Campbell. Anyone that started with an *M*. I knew I was innocent and I was almost as certain that McGovern was, so, as I told the cops repeatedly, Campbell was obviously hoist on his own petard, rubbed out by some faction of his own mob-style killers. You lives by the watermelon, you dies by the watermelon.

The cops weren't buying any watermelon, however. Nor were they buying any red herrings. I carefully avoided using that expression during my interview with them so as not to increase my amateur standing in their eyes, but privately I felt more and more certain that Campbell's death was unrelated to the other two and that if some break didn't come very quickly, Campbell's death was going to be unrelated to the other three. Because there would probably be another croaking. Trouble was, I didn't have any idea who the croakee was going to be. I did have an idea about the identity of the croaker but it wasn't the kind of thing the cops would take seriously if I told them. It wasn't the kind of thing anybody would take seriously.

By the time Bill Johnson came to the phone, I'd almost forgotten who the hell he was and Peter Myers was hallooing me from the sidewalk below. I told Bill Johnson to wait, threw down the puppet head to Myers, and then proceeded to explain to Johnson my close working relationship with the police and my immediate need for a tape copy of the voice of the deceased.

'Frank Worthington, you say? Couldn't forget him. Horrible thing to happen . . .'

'Terrible,' I said.

'I'm sure we have a tape somewhere,' he said. 'When do you need it?'

'Yesterday, pal,' I said, 'yesterday.'

'I'll call you back within the hour,' he said.

'Roger,' I said. 'This'll make the boys at the precinct very happy.' You couldn't lay it on too thick for these advertising guys. In fact, you had to lay it on pretty thick because their skulls were so thick.

'I've brought you something,' said Myers as he came in the door to my loft. I retrieved the puppet head from him and put it back on top of the refrigerator. You never know who might come calling on you these days. Best to be prepared.

Myers took a small, round, hard object about the size of a hockey puck out of a paper bag he was carrying. He set it down squarely in the middle of the kitchen table.

'Know what that is?' he asked.

'Somebody's lost their hockey puck,' I said. Myers laughed heartily. He sounded like some kind of British Sten gun. 'That's good! That's good!' he said.

'Yeah, it's pretty goddamn funny.' This guy was too much.

'You Americans are too much,' he said. 'This is a pork pie. You do eat pork, don't you?'

'No. Our leader, Mohammed, forbids it.'

'Pity.'

'Listen, pal,' I said, 'I've got a busy weekend ahead and I got no time for small talk. I'm going to make you a nice cup of tea and I want you to sit down here and spill it and I don't mean the tea.' I made Myers a cup of tea. I even made myself a cup of tea so I could be on the same wavelength with him.

I got the teacups, sugar, cream and Myers in place around the table, and I went over and picked up the shrink's report off the desk. I sat down across from Myers, who was taking tentative little sips of his tea and making little expressions like somebody was jabbing him with a hatpin.

'Well,' I said, 'everybody's here but the Mad Hatter. He, apparently, couldn't make it today but we do have his confidential shrink report. It requires a great leap of faith but I'll assume, only for the sake of discussion, you understand, that you did not kill Frank Worthington.'

'Big of you,' he said.

'Yes. Now, you see that at the beginning of the shrink's notes,

Worthington is discussing his troubled relationship with "C". Then we flip a few pages and Worthington flips out a few more times and we come to somebody named "N." Now toward the end of the whole megillah we have mention of a character referred to as "M." That would be you, my lad, correct?'

'Whatever you say.'

'So if we draw a flow chart on a Carnegie Delicatessen napkin, we go back a little over four years to "Campbell," come to "Nina Kong" about a year later, and finally, as Worthington ends therapy with this shrink about two and a half years ago, we find that he leaves his mind at your doorstep.'

Myers's upright posture had deteriorated to that of a large fishing worm. 'I didn't kill the poor blighter,' he said, 'though God knows there were times I'd have liked to.'

'Your dear departed friend Barry Campbell claims he was leaving Worthington's apartment about when you were arriving. It looks like you were among the last to see Frankie Boy alive. If not the last.'

'I didn't kill him.'

'Fine.'

'And Campbell was no friend of mine. That cunt.'

'May he rest in peace,' I said. I had disliked Campbell at least as much as Myers had, but still, it was an interesting choice of words. The British, of course, often referred derogatorily to both men and women as 'cunts.' Homosexuals used the word often too, usually but not always applying it to men and meaning about the same as when they called a man a 'bitch.' I thought suddenly of McGovern. He used the word to describe any man, woman, or child that got in his way. 'Cunt' was not a word I often used in my own vocabulary, but it was a word that would come back to haunt me before this sordid business was over.

There was only one more loose end concerning Pete Myers that I wanted to tie up before I let him go. I still had to see Johnson, the guy from the ad agency, about the tape of Worthington's voice, and I still planned to pay a visit to Nina Kong at the recording studio that night. I looked Myers right in the eye and he looked into his teacup.

'What're you doing,' I asked, 'reading the leaves?' He looked up at me sullenly. 'What else do you want?' he said.

'How many flowers did you see there at Worthington's?'

'A dozen. A dozen roses.'

'You sure, Myers?'

'Sure as I could be. I left my abacus at home, you see.' He was one smug item.

'Just one more thing, Myers. What did Darlene Rigby want from you when she called you just before midnight on the night she was murdered?'

He looked right at me and he didn't bat an eye. Then he smiled and he leaned back in his chair.

'She wanted my recipe for pork pies,' he said.

## 42

Just before five o'clock that evening I went by Umbrella, Inc., to pick up the tape I'd ordered. You don't get to be head of an advertising agency in New York by being a nice guy but Johnson wasn't too bad for a guy in a three-piece suit. If I'd had to dress that way every day for the past twenty years, I probably wouldn't have been much better.

I walked out of there twenty minutes later with a cassette and a smile. I thought I had friends in the advertising business and Johnson thought he had friends at the Sixth Precinct. So much for friendship.

I called Ratso at his office to find out when he'd be back at the loft. I wanted to get his opinion of the tapes.

When I finally got through to him he said, 'Dr Felch. Is that you?'

'Yeah. When are you going to be at the loft?'

'Can you give me half an hour?' he asked.

'I can give you a lot longer than that, pal.'

'Okay, don't get snippy. I'll be there a little after six.'

I stopped off at a little grocery on the corner and did my shopping for the week. Cigars, coffee, cat food, toilet paper. I also bought some wine, cheese, and a rather vile-looking Italian sausage. You never knew when you were going to have guests. As I was ankling it up Vandam, I noticed a cab pulled over to the side of the street with the driver's door open. The driver was standing behind the door taking a leak on the street and it was too late to pretend I hadn't seen him.

'How's it going?' I said. He didn't answer but he did give me a little sneer. This kind of thing happened quite often on Vandam. It was a quiet street but you paid the price in other ways. I couldn't blame the guy. I'd been there myself. If you didn't have a wad of bills, credit cards, and a hotel key, you were going to have a hell of a time trying to urinate in New York. It was easier to cop a plea than it was to cop a pee.

By the time I got home Ratso was already there, screwdriver in hand, cursing the television set.

'I'll tell you, Sherlock, the sacrifices I make for you.'

'Not everybody has Manhattan Cable, pal. Now you see how the other half lives.' I put the groceries away, such as they were, and poured a mean jigger of Jameson into the bull's horn shot glass. The cat had a late brunch so I didn't bother with feeding her just then. She wasn't knocked out about it, I could tell, but she took it stoically. On balance, she was handling herself better than Ratso.

'Come over here, Rat, I want you to hear something. This is bachelor number one,' I said as I rewound and played back the tape on my answering machine. We heard again the same sober, anomic voice: 'This is Frank Worthington . . .'

I popped the cassette out and put in the one that Johnson had given me. 'Now this is bachelor number two.' The voice we heard was vibrant this time and decidedly earth-bound, but there was no mistaking its identity. It said, 'Are you a hemorrhoid sufferer? If you are, this message is for you. Painful, inflamed hemorrhoidal tissues . . .'

'Enough!' shouted Ratso. 'No question about it.'

'I agree,' I said. 'Bachelor number one and bachelor number two are clearly the same person.'

We had a match all right but it looked like a match that had been made in hell.

'Well,' said Ratso, 'if Worthington is dead, which we know he is, why in the hell is he still calling us?'

'There are certain other possibilities that suggest themselves, my dear Ratso,' I said, as I put on my hunting vest and reached for a few cigars.

'Where are you going?' he asked.

'Out,' I said. 'The game is afoot.'

I wasn't sure who the game was or what the game was. All I knew was I was going to try to bite it before it bit me.

## 43

I walked down Eighth Street on my way to the studio where Nina Kong was finishing her rock video. It was Friday night again, exactly two weeks to the day since Frank Worthington had gotten himself croaked and had gotten me into this ungodly mess. As I walked I took stock of the situation. No one had been croaked now in almost twenty-four hours. That was saying something. Maybe this was the end of it, but I really didn't believe it. The more I thought about it, the less likely I thought it was that Worthington and Rigby's killer had murdered Campbell. For one thing, Campbell's death looked like a garden-variety hit to me. It wasn't cute. Where was the flair? Where was the killer's sense of humor? No, Campbell's death had come about because he was getting too big for his stylish little suspendered britches. Maybe I indirectly helped his demise. Maybe he was snuffed out by a couple of disgruntled haircuts in aluminum suits. It just didn't fit with the other two croakings. I didn't see the fine Italian hand.

I wasn't through with Myers, I was just getting ready to tackle Nina, and tomorrow I intended to put what Adrian was pleased to call her mind through a Deering blender. If she was squirreling anything, I was sure as hell going to find out. Earlier in the day, before Myers and I had had our little tea party, I'd spoken to Cynthia. It hadn't been an easy call to make. She was already in the throes of a deep depression. I told her that time was running out, that I'd be talking to everybody involved this weekend, including herself. I told her to brace up as best she could and keep her powder dry. Better yet, I said, avoid the powder, avoid Adrian if possible, and be damn careful about letting any information slip to her. Adrian was a cocaine dealer, not a father confessor. I also invited Cynthia to join me for dinner Sunday night at the Derby.

That was about where things stood when I half trampled a Moonie who was selling flowers in the middle of the sidewalk at Eight and University. He never stopped smiling all the way to the pavement. Bouquets of flowers all wrapped neatly in cellophane fell to the sidewalk, too. That was how you could always tell a Moonie – lots of smiling and lots of cellophane. I didn't hate Moonies but I didn't like them either, so I just kept walking and the Moonie just kept smiling. Never even said 'Watch where you're going.' But I figured I'd better watch where I was going anyway, because where I was going there lurked a psycho killer just waiting to make me a part of a nice burgeoning little corpse collection.

They say the grass is always greener over a corpse but I certainly wasn't dying to find out if it was true.

I gave my name to the Philip Morris midget at the door of the building and he waved me into the elevator. Four floors and one crushed cigar stub later, I strolled into the studio lobby where hordes of hangers-on were milling about and walked up to what looked to be the mission-control desk. The guy behind the desk had an inflated opinion of his own importance, but anybody could have developed that just by being exposed to the flotsam and jetsam drifting around the rest of the lobby.

'Who the hell are these people?' I asked the guy.

'They're the "audience" we're using for the video. Who wants to know?' he said.

'I think I've spoken to you before, pal,' I said. 'It wasn't overly pleasant that time either.' I gave him my name.

'Oh, yeah,' he said, 'I remember you said you were some kind of booking agent last time you called.' This guy obviously wasn't a Moonie. If he was, he sure wasn't smiling too much.

'Anything's possible,' I said. 'Where can I find Nina?'

'Right through that door,' he said, pointing into the studio. 'She's working on close-ups now, but she wants to talk to you.'

I walked through the soundproofed double doors of the recording studio into a room filled with acrid yellow smoke and hot lights. The guys with the smoke pellets were working overtime. A couple of video types were directing operations. From the way they acted, you'd think they were directing a crowd scene in some mammoth biblical epic. Well, we all had our dreams.

The music was loud and unintelligible. Even McGovern wouldn't have liked it. And the same eight bars or so were being repeated over and over at top decibel level. I'd been in worse places, but this one was certainly in the running. It wasn't a bad approximation of my idea of hell.

My eyes were beginning to clear a little bit and I could see that there was a sound stage with some people on it. One of them was Nina Kong. One of the makeup crew was dusting Nina's face with a little powder, but her face wasn't the most interesting part of Nina. I squinted my eyes to be sure I was seeing things right. I was.

It didn't take a pair of opera glasses to tell that Nina Kong was dressed entirely as a man.

## 44

We were in a posh little room off to one side of the sound stage. It had low lighting, comfortable furniture, soundproofed walls, and a good lock on the door. It looked as if it had been designed for what Nina was doing, which was laying out a pretty fair quantity of cocaine onto a large glass tabletop.

'That's a lot of fish ice cream you got there,' I said.

'Is it?' she said without taking her eyes off her work.

'Before we burn too many synapses here, why did you lie to me about not knowing Barry Campbell?'

'I was hoping you wouldn't ask any hard questions. It's a long story,' she said. Her upper lip was trembling a little as she lowered a nicely shaped nostril in for a landing onto the glass tabletop.

'Try to nut-shell it,' I said.

'I wouldn't know where to start,' she said.

'Start with why you lied to me about Campbell.' I started to bring a nostril in for a landing myself but hesitated and made a last minute flyover instead. The tower told me to circle for a while.

'I knew Barry. Of course I knew Barry. I didn't tell you for two reasons. One was that I loved him once. And the other was that I thought he'd killed Frank. At least up until last night I thought he'd killed Frank.' I watched as a few more light planes came in. She knew how to handle an aircraft all right. Of course, there wasn't much chance of missing the field, but still, a case of pilot error could be pretty expensive.

'I've been lonely most of my life,' she said. I brought in a big transcontinental Concorde. The kind with its nose pointed down. 'My parents were never able to show me that they loved me . . .'

'You know what this is?' I asked. I was moving the index finger of my left hand back and forth across the thumbnail of the same hand.

'No,' she said. She was sulking and she looked great when she sulked. Just sitting there pouting with that little tie on and dressed as a man she was something to see. Maybe I was subconsciously a homosexual. I'd have to ask Dr Bock when he got back.

'You don't know what this is?' I said. 'Well, let me tell you, honey. It's the smallest violin in the world and it's playing "Hearts and Flowers." '

'You're an insensitive prick, you know that?'

'Mr Insensitive Prick to you, honey,' I said. 'Pray continue and don't let anything I might say ruffle your beautiful feathers. Life is tough and it's a funny old world and I just don't feel sorry for you. I've seen people who clean their teeth with steel wool in Vermont.' I felt like grudge-jumping her right there on the spot but I thought better of it.

'It's not something I'm exactly proud of. Barry and I both were involved with Frank. First me and then Barry.'

'Jesus,' I said. 'Frank dumped you for Barry.' No wonder Worthington was seeing a shrink.

'That's a nice way of putting it,' she said.

'Go on,' I said. The jets were starting to come in on the little landing strip. Air traffic was getting pretty heavy.

'Frank dumped Barry, as you say, for Pete, though I don't think Pete was that interested. Barry and I were both rebounders. But when a woman is rejected by a man for another man, something happens to her. I'd never had much love in my life and I sort of went off the deep end. It was a low point for me. It hit me really hard. Barry picked me up and I'll always be grateful to him for it. I was rebounding terribly, and then he was rebounding, and we both just sort of rebounded together at a crucial period for me. Later we drifted apart and went our own ways but I've never forgotten. Maybe you don't know what it's like. Maybe you've never been a rebounder.'

'Everybody's a rebounder, honey,' I said. 'If there weren't any rebounding in this world, there'd be one hell of a lot of missed hoops.' I was such a wise, understanding person.

I wanted to hug her but I took a Carnegie Delicatessen napkin out of my pocket instead. 'Look at this,' I said.

'So what?' she said. 'So he makes a goooood sandwich?'

I looked at the napkin. There was a little cartoon logo of my friend Carnegie Leo holding up a big pastrami sandwich and saying his famous slogan: 'I make a goooood sandwich.'

'That's not what I meant,' I said. 'Look over here.' I showed her the flow chart of Frank Worthington's bisexual history as Dr Bock had recorded it. On the napkin I'd written the following: C.-N.-M.

She studied the three initials for a moment and then said: 'No, that's wrong. It should read: N.-C.-M.'

'Okay,' I said. 'Nina, Campbell, Myers.' I put the changed order of the initials underneath the old grouping.

'Curious,' I said.

'Is that supposed to be a clue or something?' she asked in a pose of sexy mock innocence that was really quite fetching, I thought.

'No,' I said, 'it's in case you spill something on your tie. That's a nice outfit, kid.' She blushed a little or maybe the blood was just rushing to her head.

'You wouldn't dress like that out on the street, would you?' I asked. 'Out on Jane Street?'

' "No" is the answer to both your questions. I'm shy.'

'That's funny; you don't look shy.'

'I'm shy,' she continued as if I hadn't interrupted. 'I'm dressing like this for the video. I'm not some kind of dyke, if that's what you think. I did not kill Frank Worthington. I'm sad about Barry and I'm sorry about that actress girl whatever her name was . . .'

'You sound it.'

'I am sorry, damn it,' she said and she stamped her little foot. She looked, in spite of her clothing, like a woman through and through and she looked dangerous as hell. 'I'm not sorry Frank was killed,' she said as an afterthought.

'Yeah,' I said, 'he was a pretty popular guy all around.'

'Look,' she said, 'I've got to get back in there for about ninety-seven more hours of close-ups. You do some of this special stuff.' She took out the little ceramic snuffbox that I'd seen before in the limousine. My hands weren't trembling yet, so I thought I'd go ahead and give it a try.

'Knock yourself out,' she said.

'I wish you hadn't said that,' I said. 'I was just starting to like you again.'

She shrugged; then she smiled and went over and opened the door. As we walked back toward the sound stage, she suddenly took my hand and led me into a little empty hallway somewhere behind the stage. She turned and I was aware that she was standing very close to me. We grabbed each other at about the same time, and I held her for a moment very tightly. If anyone on the street could have seen us, they would probably have thought nothing of two men standing together with their bodies caught up in a passionate embrace. 'What do you expect?' they would have said. 'It's the Village.'

After a moment or two I whispered to her. 'Don't say "Knock yourself out," honey.'

'Don't say anything,' she whispered. I didn't.

Later, after I'd straightened her tie and I'd said good-bye to her in the little hallway, I was walking out toward the lobby when she called after me. 'I could be getting jealous,' she said. 'Ever find out who sent you that rose?'

'Yeah,' I said, 'I think I have.'

## 45

Saturday morning broke colder than The Weasel's smile. It was snowing outside and the falling flakes reminded me that I had to call Adrian. Ratso was still asleep on the couch, so I made some coffee and the cat and I sat by the window and watched the snow fall while I screwed up my nerve to hear Adrian's voice in the morning.

She was the kind of girl that older dentists find attractive. She had a nice set of teeth, a fair set of knockers, and a lousy set of values. She was a chemical puppet. I could picture her now after a night of wheeling, dealing, and tooting her own horn, out cold on the couch in some parody of a lingerie getup that even the perviest guy in the universe wouldn't find too exciting. Perrier spilled all over the floor probably. A few pieces of pizza spot-welded upside down on the couch next to her.

Well, like they said about the guy who stabbed his wife thirty-seven times with a screwdriver, nobody's perfect.

I called Adrian. I let the phone ring about nine times and hung up. Maybe she'd disconnected it. I frankly doubted that she was out bird-watching in Central Park.

It was now 10.00 a.m. I gave Mick Brennan a ring.

'Umhmmmm . . .' said Brennan.

'Leap sideways, pal,' I said. 'I need that information I asked you for. No later than this afternoon. Ask Bob Miller. Ask around in the city room. I've got to have it and fast.'

I hung up and called the little florist shop on Hudson Street. When I had called two weeks earlier, a young girl had been working there. She'd been very sweet and cooperative, checking the ledger and informing me that it was Barry Campbell who'd ordered the flowers for Frank Worthington. Now, two weeks later, the phone was answered by a mean old lady who didn't sound like she'd give me the time of day. Maybe the young girl had grown up.

It was not a pleasant phone call. The old lady bitched. I badgered. I threatened. She cackled. I cajoled. She grudgingly gave.

Worthington's flowers had gone out at 9.45 a.m. First delivery of the day.

'Are you satisfied now?' she asked smugly. 'Do you want to place an order?'

'Yeah, lady,' I said. 'I want to order you to hang up your telephone.'

I tried Adrian's number again. No answer. I walked back over to the window. The cat was still sitting on the sill. The garbage trucks looked very tranquil in the snow. A few big flakes drifted against the windowpane and the cat observed them with deep curiosity. I didn't know whether the cat could see the pattern in the snowflakes or not, but I was finally starting to see a few patterns myself. And what I saw I didn't like.

It was crowding 11.30. The snow was still falling, the cat was still watching, and Ratso and I were having an espresso at the kitchen table. Much to Ratso's displeasure, I was smoking my first cigar of the day and the smoke all seemed to be drifting directly into his left eye. There was nothing I could do about it.

I took out my old napkin from the Carnegie Delicatessen and spread it on the table in front of Ratso. 'I want to show you something. Do you know what this means?'

'What's it mean?' he asked. 'You don't get linen anymore?' He was referring to the Carnegie's tradition of giving linen napkins to their special customers. When a celebrity or a favorite customer came into the place, Carnegie Leo would shout to the waiter, 'Give 'em linen.' So you'd sit at a big table with the guy on your right and the guy on your left using paper napkins and you had linen. It was one of the few true rushes left in life.

I explained to Ratso the first little chart that I'd made according to the shrink's notes, and then I showed him the second one underneath it that was Nina Kong's version.

'Curious,' he said.

'That's what I said,' I said. I wasn't even sure that Nina's elevator went to the top floor, but if it did and her version was correct, it raised a rather unaccountable discrepancy. We decided to talk it over at lunch and what better place to have it than at the Carnegie.

I left the cat in charge, and we walked along in the crisp, white snow through the Village for a while. It was a beautiful village. Especially when it was blanketed with newly fallen snow. Of course, give it about two hours and it would look like crankcase oil. But beauty never lasts in this world. God and man and large dogs see to that.

We took a cab up to Fifty-fifth and Seventh and joined the long line waiting for tables inside the Carnegie Delicatessen. Leo spotted us in the line, pulled us out, found a table for us, and told the head waiter, 'Give 'em linen.' We ordered two bowls of matzo-ball soup. Ratso stuffed his linen napkin into the neck of his shirt so the neighboring diners couldn't miss it. We had a couple of pastrami sandwiches, which Leo claims are the best in New York and he won't get a beef from me about it. We had some seltzer, Dr Brown's Creme Soda, coffee, cheesecake, and Ratso topped things off by ordering a pope's nose. The waiter said he'd ask the guy at the counter if they had one. They did. It was the rear end of a turkey. Quite a delicacy in deli circles, I'm told.

We did not discuss the case and I didn't think about McGovern once until we got home and there was a message on the machine from Mick Brennan. I rang him up right away.

'Spit it, Mick,' I said.

'It's just as you thought,' he said. 'Friday morning around eleven o'clock was one time. That wasn't the only occasion either. But I still don't see what it means.'

'These are deep waters, Brennan. And at the bottom lurks a creature that's going to make the Loch Ness Monster look like a cute little ET. Say nothing about this to anyone if you value your life.'

'Right, mate.'

'Even if you don't value your life,' I added as an afterthought. It was hard to tell sometimes with Mick.

I knew how the murderer had committed the crime. I had the timing down now. I could even see the motive beginning to crystallize in the back of my mind. All I needed was for the mask of death to drop and show the even deadlier face behind it.

## 46

By ten o'clock Saturday night the Monkey's Paw was beginning to twitch pretty good. Outside, the snow was still on the ground, but if you'd built a snowman out of it, he would've died of toxic poisoning. I was standing by the bar nursing a Guinness and quietly piecing together a mosaic of murder in my mind. I was playing a cat-and-mouse game with myself and it was proving to be an exasperating experience. I was the cat. Whoever or whatever the mouse was I couldn't quite tell, but it was peeping at me from every dusty corner of my mind. Several times as I stood there, I thought I had him, but he always managed to scurry away just beyond the reach of my memory. Damn! Six more inches and I would have been king.

This little mental mouse I was chasing through the rusty convolutions of my brain had something to do with drugs, something to do with the voice of a dead man whom I'd never met, something . . . something else . . . but it was gone again . . . like a ghost in a hallway . . .

I'd have to talk this over with my cat when I got home. What would the cat do if it were in my place? How do you catch a mouse when you're not even sure it's really there?

I ordered another Guinness from Tommy, who was not smiling like a Moonie. He looked a little harassed tonight. I wasn't experiencing the even-mindedness of the ol' Mahatma myself. I reached through a well-dressed young Saturday night couple for the Guinness.

'Pardon my boardinghouse reach,' I said.

'Don't mention it, chief,' said the guy.

'Fine.'

The second Guinness was bringing out the mouse a little better. I had to go on the assumption that McGovern was the victim of a fiendishly clever frame-up. Of course, I could be wrong about that. Invariably the neighbors of mass murderers were wrong about them. So were their teachers, parents, gym coaches, best friends. Maybe it took a psycho to know a psycho. Maybe I was such a wonderful trusting American that I'd had McGovern lamped wrong the whole time.

As my old friend Slim used to say back in Texas, 'You never know what the monkey eat until the monkey shit.' Crude, but appropriate. Possibly very appropriate.

When I got heavily monstered I could often remember things I thought I couldn't remember. For example, I had repressed many things in my past. One of them was California. But when I got truly hammered, sometimes I could vividly recall just about every loving, bloody, Technicolor detail of Yesterday Street. I could reel off the phone numbers of hotels in LA and Santa Monica, of half-a-dozen long-forgotten coke dealers, of old girlfriends and lost loves who'd gone on to whatever they go on to. Probably making a mess of some other guy's life. Did they stop a second to think of me as they stood in the patio with the kids all around and the husband standing by the barbecue pit? I hoped not.

I could even speak fluent Malay and a little Swahili when I was drunk.

'Uh-oh, here comes trouble,' said a familiar voice with a thick British accent.

'*Hujambo, bwana,*' I said. It was Mick Brennan, and from the look of him he'd already covered Yesterday Street like a Fuller brush man.

'What're you doing tomorrow night, mate? We're having some roast beef with Yorkshire pudding over at a friend's place. We need a token American.'

'Can't,' I said. 'I'm taking Cynthia to the Derby.'

'Ah,' he said, 'while the bloody cat's away the bleeding mice will play, eh?'

'Closer than you know, pal.'

'Cheers,' he said and ordered another round for us.

'Where is he tonight, Mick?' I asked.

'Who? McGovern or The Weasel?'

'I already don't know where McGovern is,' I said. 'I'm talkin' Weasel, man. Where is that miserable little porch monkey?'

'He was here earlier but he left. Said he wouldn't be back tonight. Looked to be a bit upset. Said he thought his source had dried up.'

'Jesus,' I said. On instinct I went to the pay phone, dropped a quarter, and dialed Adrian's number. There was no answer. I let it ring about eleven times but I wasn't really listening anymore.

It fit together too well. It probably had been going on for years and I hadn't known. Hadn't even guessed. But now I knew as surely as I was standing there with the receiver in my hand.

The Weasel had been getting his stuff from Adrian.

All the time it had been literally right under my nose.

## 47

It was with a certain chill of premonition that I hailed a cab up Fourth Street to Adrian's place. Many thoughts were suddenly hurtling through my mind and none of them was 'Have a nice day.' I didn't have the key with me to the building on 42 Jane Street, but there was no time to go back to the loft to get it. Adrian hadn't answered the phone from the first time I'd tried her at ten o'clock that morning until just minutes ago when I'd called again from the Monkey's Paw.

That was a long time between dreams.

Especially for a coke dealer who rarely left her apartment. Maybe she was visiting her mother in Teaneck. Or her brother in Redneck. Did coke dealers have mothers or brothers? I supposed it was possible. I knew The Weasel didn't have a mother in Teaneck. The rock he'd crawled out from under was on the third ring of Saturn.

Career coke dealers had no real friends in the world; why should they have family? The architecture of their lives came down to nothing but straws and mirrors. They were spinning ghosts in the land of the lost . . . spinning ghosts . . .

It would have been a hell of a lot faster if I'd hoofed it up Fourth, I now realized. The Saturday night Village traffic was a honking, crawling nightmare in itself. But it gave me a little chance to think.

I noticed there wasn't any 'No Smoking' sign in the cab so I reached into my old hunting vest and came up with a good two-dollar and twenty-five-cent Partagas cigar. What this country needed was a good two-dollar and twenty-five-cent cigar. That and a couple of other things.

I lit the cigar and I leaned back on the seat and puffed a bit. I thought of what I might find at my journey's end.

'You smoke the cigar?' asked the driver. 'No smoking the cigar,' he shouted. 'No smoke!'

'Fine,' I said. The cigar cost more than the goddamn fare. I got out in the middle of the street and paid the guy, giving him a tip that was appropriate to the services.

I'd just about decided that it wouldn't pay to go rushing into Adrian's place as if I expected something to be amiss. For one thing, it was just possible the cops might be there already. For another, the neighbors might see me and tell the cops a guy with a big cigar was running through the building after midnight and that he wasn't Ernie Kovacs. And for a third thing, maybe nothing at all was amiss and my whole intrusion would just amount to a social embarrassment. I could survive dropping the salad fork.

So I slowed my pace a little. But just a little.

I walked past the Corner Bistro and I saw the little thatched roof on top of the green windmill across from 42 Jane Street. I stood and looked at the building where McGovern had lived and had first seen Frank Worthington's ghost. Where Frank Worthington had lived and died a violent death. I hoped that Adrian, whatever tense she was currently in, wasn't there. Not that she and I went way back or anything; I just hoped she wasn't there. I hoped she was attending a coke-dealers convention this weekend in Vail, Colorado, and had forgotten to mention it to anyone.

Like the commercial for Holiday Inn, I wanted no surprises.

I looked both ways before crossing the street. It was a little trick I'd learned in Singapore. There was nobody on the street at all unless you wanted to count the kid on the bicycle or the guy going through the garbage cans. It was a quiet reflective moment in the life of Jane Street before the lights changed or the bars closed. I crossed the street.

I climbed the four steps, opened the door into the little hallway, found Adrian's buzzer, and leaned heavily on it. I listened for a voice but it was quiet as a picnic in the country. Quiet as a funeral in the suburbs. It was so quiet it almost made you want to scream. It was deadly quiet.

I stepped back out to the sidewalk to get some air and to test my auditory responses. Maybe I'd hear a guy arguing with his wife. Maybe a car going by or a junkie walking down the sidewalk talking to himself. Maybe even a garbage truck . . . Nothing. It was the same frightening sensation you'd get if you were walking in the jungle and suddenly all the birds stopped singing. You knew the leopard was going to pounce; you just didn't know which shadow it was going to pounce from. And at times like these you wouldn't really be considering whether or not the leopard had changed its spots. I certainly wasn't.

I scrambled back up the steps and practiced a little Morse code on McGovern's buzzer. With any luck Cynthia would be there. Nothing . . . Where the hell was Rambam when you needed him? Where was anybody when you needed him?

I walked over to the Bistro. I even had a hard time getting the bartender. The Bistro was jumping on a Saturday night.

'Dave,' I shouted. 'Dave! Give me a shot of something.'

'Right you are,' said Dave and he gave me a shot of something. It tasted like some Benedictine monk had forgotten to put the cork back on it for a couple of years but I wasn't going to complain. I went to the pay phone, which cringed on the wall next to the blaring jukebox, and I did my best to call Cynthia's number. She wasn't home but Southside Johnny was. I ordered another shot of whatever it was I'd ordered the first time, and it tasted better the second time. Kind of like love except it was cheaper.

I went back to 42 Jane and pushed Adrian's buzzer – more nothing. I camped out on Cynthia's buzzer for a while. I practically pushed the damn thing through the wall and I kept repeating

'Cynthia' in a loud voice that was beginning to sound like a guy pulling the starter cord on a busted lawn mower. At last I heard a small voice and I didn't think it sounded like my conscience.

'Yes. Who is it?' it said.

'Cynthia, it's me. For Christ's sake, let me in.' The door buzzed and I pushed the damn thing open and went up to McGovern's. Cynthia was alive and well and apparently just getting out of the shower.

'I was just taking a shower,' she said. 'Was that you on the telephone too?'

'Yeah.' She was wearing a housecoat with red and blue parrots that looked as if they were about to fall off their perch. I was about to fall off mine too, only I didn't know it at the time.

'I'm going upstairs in a second; got a shot of something?' I asked. Some women were at their very best coming out of the shower. She looked troubled and damp and ravishing. But it was a rather obvious case of time does not allow. And then there was the specter of McGovern lurking out there somewhere in the night. There was also my growing dread of whatever the hell I might find upstairs. But that was another story.

Cynthia brought me the drink. It was better than the Bistro's and the service was too. I caught a quick glimpse of myself in the bathroom mirror and I knew I needed a bracer. I looked like the loneliest man I'd ever met. I looked like an out patient who needed to get back in.

I downed the rest of the drink. 'Thanks,' I said. 'Have you seen Adrian?'

'Not since two days ago. No. I haven't seen her.'

'Well, don't hold your breath. Stay here – I'll be right back. I'm going up.' I didn't want to leave Cynthia and about half of me didn't want to know what was up there on the third floor, so I kissed Cynthia on the forehead and lightly over her closed eyes. She kissed me on the lips and held on to me for dear life.

'I've got to get up there,' I said and I took her arms from around my neck and held her in front of me until I could see the parrots real well. 'I'll be right back,' I told her, and I went out the door and up the stairs to the third floor.

A couple of those parrots had looked like they wanted a cracker bad, and they didn't look like they really cared whether or not that cracker was me.

## 48

I knocked on Adrian's door not like I was expecting any answer but like I was checking to see if the room was hollow. It wasn't. But it was dark as some unlit corner of hell. The door had opened much too easily for my blood.

My hand crept along the wall for the light switch and the flesh crept along the back of my neck. I didn't know where it was creeping to but I wished it would stop. It didn't. I found the switch and I hit the lights. I blinked a few times and took a step forward. I was almost on top of her before I saw her. She was lying facedown on the floor right between the light green sofa and the dark green coffee table. I turned her over and her face was a bad lavender.

She was colder than a frozen margarita. There were little bubbles of foam still clinging to the corners of her mouth. Her eyes were caught in the act of trying to tell something to someone, only whoever the someone had been, he was gone and I wasn't. Not that I didn't want to be gone. I wanted to goose-step right out of there, but I forced myself to stick around like an unwanted guest at a party of one.

Adrian was the second stiff I'd seen in this building in just a little over a fortnight. It was a case of history starting to cause ennui. Served me right for not staying at the Holiday Inn.

As I stood up and took a step backward, something made a little crunching sound under my left foot. When I picked it up, I saw that it was a small fragment of pink glass. I looked around on the floor and found a few more pieces in several pastel colors that reminded me of something. Oh, Christ. It was what was left of Adrian's poor, pathetic pane of stained glass. Someone had done a pretty thorough job of smashing it all to hell, and it hadn't been a kid with a baseball. The girl had spent an eternity working on her own little masterpiece and the only gallery it would ever see was this floor of dusty death. Art imitating life. And life was the strangest monkey of them all.

It was enough to bring a tear to a stained-glass eye.

I looked down at the coffee table for the first time. There was maybe half an ounce of cocaine swirled out across the coffee table in the stark, determined configurations of a word. The clumsy white letters against the green background were vaguely reminiscent of the scribblings of a child on a blackboard someone had erased along with the other fragile memories of forgotten youth.

But this writing was not the work of a child. One word was written in cocaine on top of the little table.

The word was 'Cunt.'

'So that's the story, Sergeant. I haven't pinched anything but my own arm to see if I was dreaming.' There were three of us in the room – Sergeant Fox, myself, and Adrian's stiff – and I seemed to be the one who'd been doing most of the talking. 'So it's getting late and I'd like to check out the alibis of a few Americans before the trail gets too cold. Can I talk to you guys in the morning?'

'Jesus, you country-singer types are something, aren't you?' said Fox, as he picked up a small sliver of stained glass with his handkerchief.

'I'm not a country-singer type anymore,' I said. 'Now I'm in the the-ah-tuh.' I gave Fox the most friendly, engaging smile I could find in the warehouse. He just kept studying the piece of glass like it was the key to everything man didn't know in the world. Maybe it was. If anybody had come into the room, it would have looked like he was holding a tiny piece of ice in his handkerchief and seeing how long it would take for it to melt. It reminded me of Bat Masterson's last comment on life. He had been a sportswriter on the New York *Morning Telegraph*, and his colleagues had found the following message in his typewriter after he died: 'I have found the secret of life. It is ice. The poor folks have it in the winter and the rich folks have it in the summer.'

The poor folks evidently had it now because it was as cold as a warlock's nipple outside. And inside the apartment building at 42 Jane Street, you couldn't get much poorer than poor Adrian.

'Poisoned,' said Fox, as he walked across the room and stopped at the coffee table. 'Either in the Perrier or maybe cut right into the product here. Poisoned cocaine. A poison within a poison.' He looked at the four-letter word on the coffee table. 'That's nice,' he said.

'Yeah, I thought you'd like that,' I said. 'Look, I think I'll be going now. I forgot to feed the cat.'

'You're staying with me, pal,' he said. 'We're gonna get real close before this thing's over. If one of us eats a piece of watermelon, the other one's gonna be able to spit out the seeds.'

Before I could say anything else – not that there was much to say – Cooperman came hustling into the room. When he saw me he didn't know whether to shit or go blind.

But he recovered nicely. 'Goddamn, Fox, this guy's a regular advance man. The longer it takes to find McGovern, the better this guy looks to me. But I don't think it'll take that long to find McGovern. Not after what his broad's been telling me downstairs. Come on down for a minute. I want you to hear this.'

The police photographer and the print man had arrived and were setting up. A uniformed cop was at the door. It was one-thirty in the morning. Adrian was wearing high heels, a rather risqué, black, see-through-but-you-wish-you-hadn't sort of negligee affair. She was also wearing a very twisted, cyanide smile. She would not be dealing tonight. She was in for the evening forever.

Cynthia was sitting on McGovern's big stuffed easy chair and looking very fragile. She'd been crying, she'd been drinking a little, and I didn't know what else she'd been doing. Fox was standing over her with one foot on the radiator, which, as usual, was cold. Cooperman was standing by the fireplace warming himself by the nonexistent fire. I gathered a few old newspapers from McGovern's own personal morgue that threatened to block out what little sunlight ever crept into his living room, then grabbed a few small logs and made like a boy scout for a few minutes.

Soon I had a fair approximation of a fire going. It wouldn't have warmed the hearts or the hands of a band of gypsies, but by New York standards it wasn't bad.

I walked into the kitchen and made a drink for myself. Cynthia already had one. Fox and Cooperman weren't drinking; they were reconstructing the past twenty-four hours with Cynthia's help. It looked like it was going to be a long night.

I couldn't help but wonder if we were doing the right thing standing here yapping with Cynthia about McGovern and Adrian and letting The Weasel weasel away. And had Nina been working in the studio the past twenty-four hours? And had Pete Myers been busy cooking pork pies or had he been doing something else? It would all have to be checked out.

'Now, Miss Floyd, would you go over again what you told us earlier about what happened late last night?' It was Cooperman asking the questions as if he were talking to a child. Cooperman was taking his time. He was putting down roots there right in front of the fireplace, preparing for the long assault on Cynthia's defenses.

As it happened, it wasn't going to take the hordes of foot soldiers, the catapults, or the battering ram to get results. Cynthia's castle was already crumbling. Tears were coming again. Fox gave her a handkerchief. I hoped he'd remembered to take the piece of glass out of it first.

'Well, last night I just couldn't sleep,' said Cynthia. 'It was about two o'clock in the morning and I was just sitting here listening to the r-radio.' I wandered over to the little kitchen while she was talking and made like I was looking for a drink in the cabinets. There were two or three more little snow-seal packages tucked away in the corner of the cabinet. I tucked them a little farther away out of sight, and as long as I was already there, I pulled down a bottle of Bushmill's Irish whiskey and went through the charade of pouring a hefty jolt and drinking it. I could see why Cynthia was having trouble sleeping. I'd had trouble sleeping for years. It's hard to count sheep when you're grinding your teeth.

'I tried r-reading a book.' Cynthia was wiping her eyes with the handkerchief. 'I kept thinking about McGovern. Suddenly the door opened and he was right here in the room.'

'What time was this?' asked Cooperman.

'It was about two-thirty in the morning. I couldn't believe my eyes. I just don't want to . . . I don't want for him to . . .'

The fire crackling was the only sound in the room. I went to the kitchen and got Cynthia a brandy and walked over and gave it to her. She took it like a little girl receiving a gift.

'Cynthia,' I said, 'We know what McGovern means to you. If he's innocent, anything you say can only help to clear him. So tell us the truth. Tell us what happened last night.'

McGovern's timing was impeccably bad as usual. The guy stays away for the better part of two weeks while the whole NYPD is looking for him, and then he comes in at an ETA of almost precisely the time somebody croaks Adrian. He hadn't lost his touch.

Cynthia had stopped crying. She sniffed a few times and took a little gulp of the brandy. 'He'd been drinking and he was acting very strange. Sort of growling to himself about something. We went to bed around three in the morning and when I woke up it was already eight o'clock and he was gone. But I had had trouble falling asleep, and while I was tossing and turning, sort of half out of it, I remembered him talking, kind of snarling in his sleep. He'd done it before so I was kind of used to him talking in his sleep but this time it scared me.'

'Could you understand anything he said?' asked Cooperman.

'He was sort of cursing and growling to himself,' she said.

'And?' said Cooperman.

Silence.

'What did he say, Miss Floyd?' said Fox.

A few of the parrots had evidently gotten their feathers ruffled and she was smoothing them out. She stared down at the floor.

'Let's have it, Cynthia,' I said.

She raised her head and looked straight in front of her. Her eyes were dry and empty. She spoke in a low monotone but nobody had to ask her to repeat what she said.

'He said, "Cunt . . . cunt . . . I'll kill the cunt . . ." '

## 49

It was Sunday afternoon, bright and cold in New York. The cat, the Rat, and I were all sitting around watching Doug Flutie and the New Jersey Generals play the Arizona Heroin Addicts. USFL football was not very exciting to a lot of people and it wasn't very exciting to me either. I just liked to kind of relax, meditate, have a cup of coffee, and watch the players tump over on the field. In a world that had already lost its meaning to many folks, USFL football had to be the most meaningless facet of life on this planet. That was why I watched it.

I was heading into my third cup of coffee when the phones rang. I walked over to the desk and picked up the blower on the left. It was 3.13 p.m. It was Cooperman.

'Well, well, well,' he said. 'I've got a little news flash for you.'

'What's that? They find a cure for herpes?'

'No. But that was pretty good. Want to guess again?' I didn't like the vitality I was hearing in Cooperman's voice.

'Christ,' I said. 'I don't know. Bisexual bites dog?'

'No. It's a little hotter than that.'

'Well, what the hell is it, Sergeant?'

'Your pal McGovern turned himself in. About two hours ago. Like they say in Hollywood, it's a wrap. In fact, it's three raps. Murder One times three.'

'He didn't do it,' I said.

'Oh, yeah?' said Cooperman. 'He did it all right. And now all he's going to have to do is figure out who's going to look after his cockroaches while he's gone.'

I cradled the blower and put down the cigar I had been thinking about lighting.

Now things were starting to look bad.

Needless to say I did not take Cynthia to the Derby that Sunday night. I didn't take anybody anywhere for a long time. I didn't even take my laundry to the cleaners. I just hung around the loft adding a few layers of cigar smoke to the atmosphere in the daytime, and at night I would hit the Village bars and work a little more on developing my tavern tan.

It was like somebody had died. Not just the covey of stiffs I had hardly known who had shuffled off to Buffalo in varied and violent fashion with their name tags stuck on their big toes and who could be discussed like some sort of parlor game in a random and haphazard order. In New York nobody really regarded anybody as dead; we just thought of them as not currently working on a project.

But McGovern was somebody close to me. And McGovern was not McGovern anymore. Whether he was dead or not, I suppose, was arguable. Clinically, I knew, he was still alive somewhere in a monkey cage eating baloney sandwiches. But his mind and his spirit, I was afraid, were damn near as dead as Dumbo's mother.

I seemed to be about the only person in New York who still clung feebly to the notion that McGovern was innocent. Actually, there was another person who knew of McGovern's innocence – that was the killer. But the killer wasn't talking. The killer, having killed, had moved on to something else. He had diversified.

Weeks passed in a glum fashion. The Mets had opened their season and the Rangers had closed theirs. Ratso had been making flapping noises about flying home like a sparrow to nearby SoHo. Then one day I looked at the empty couch and I realized he was gone.

I ran into Mick Brennan a few times in the Monkey's Paw and struggled through a few rounds with him. I noticed with a perverse satisfaction that The Weasel was back in the men's room. All was well with the world.

The mills of the Lord may have been grinding slowly and they may have been grinding exceedingly fine, but I wasn't planning to use their product in my coffee machine.

## 50

One grim anonymous evening I was stroking the cat and what was left my ego when the phones rang. It was Ratso. 8.15 p.m.

'Sherlock,' he said, 'it might be a good idea if you got out a little more. Why don't we meet at Big Wong? Say about eight-forty-five.'

'Yeah,' I said. 'Okay.'

Half an hour later we were feeling as snug as two snowpeas in a pod, ordering pork lo mein, soy-sauce chicken, roast duck, and bok choy along with hot pepper sauce, duck sauce, ginger sauce, and mustard sauce. For years Big Wong's had been a mainstay for Ratso and me. It was located about halfway up Mott Street in the heart of Chinatown. We'd been there so often that, though we didn't know most of their names, the waiters were like old friends to us.

We discussed various things. Ratso's screenplay was nearing completion. My Broadway show was still on track for the fall. Ratso's job at the magazine was going along. Life was going along. Both were having some circulation problems.

We discussed women. 'There's nothing wrong with any woman that a hand grenade or a Quaalude can't straighten out,' said Ratso. I thought of how women sometimes came into our lives and left again like sleek nameless little jets equipped with heat-seeking missiles and all the latest feminine radar, landing on the decks of a creaky and battle-scarred old aircraft carrier alone in the middle of a deep and troubled sea. Sometimes the decks were clear enough for shuffleboard. Was the war over yet?

'This goddamn pork lo mein is great,' said Ratso.

'Killer bee,' I agreed.

'You know,' he said, 'it's hard to believe that an old pal could, in reality, be a psycho killer. I mean, we've known McGovern . . .'

'I don't believe it.'

'Come off it, Sherlock. You're letting your reputation lead you down the garden path. This is one time the cops are right and you are wrong, I'm sorry to say.'

'Then don't say it. Just pass the soy-sauce chicken.' Neither of us said anything for a while. The waiters poured more hot tea into our glasses and carried hot trays of food over the heads of the customers shouting all the while at the other waiters to get out of their way. The chopsticks were clicking but very little else was.

'Pass the doppelgänger lo mein, will you?' asked Ratso.

'That's cute, pal.' I signaled the waiter to drop the hatchet and a few minutes later he brought the check over.

'Of course McGovern killed those people,' said Ratso. 'He just had us going with all that ghost shit. Sort of like Son of Sam saying that his dog told him what to do. Of course there wasn't a ghost.'

Ratso performed a rather complex financial transaction involving myself, the waiter, and the guy at the cash register, which resulted in my getting screwed out of about seven dollars. It was no big deal. Three cigars.

As we left Big Wong's and walked up Mott Street to Canal, Ratso was still mumbling to himself.

'There never was any fucking ghost,' he said.

'Oh, but my dear Ratso,' I said, 'there was a ghost.'

There was also an ugly picture coming together in my attic. As we walked, some of the dust was coming off it. It was sort of an abstract work, and each time I tried to look at it, it looked like something quite different.

It was part mouse and part Japanese fishing boat. No, it wasn't a mouse. It was a weasel hiding behind a vase of flowers. There was also a mirror in the picture somewhere with a distorted face in it. It was a spectral, almost diabolical face, a witch or a demon to the superstitious eye. If I could just get out the old screwdriver and adjust the focus a little bit . . .

That night it rained like a bitch with a charge account. It let up a little around midnight, and I was feeling pretty restless so I left the cat in charge and legged it a few blocks over to the Ear. My shoulder wanted to see the place again.

'Let's get drunk and be somebody, Martin,' I said. 'There's no poetry reading tonight, is there?'

'Not on your life,' he said.

'Good.' I started with Bloody Wetbacks and Martin went a few rounds with me. The first shot of Cuervo Gold cut my throat like a bowie knife and I chased it quickly with tomato juice and a chomp of lime. Round two went better for me, and I was also looking pretty good in rounds three and four. Martin was starting to neglect his customers and some of them were yelling for service. My head was starting to feel pretty good. Kind of like a pink balloon that had gotten away from somebody at the county fair.

I thought of Nina Kong all decked out as a man in her coat and tie, leather pants, and tough guy lid. Getting dumped by Frank Worthington for another guy really twisted her head around, she'd said. I remembered the carved statues in the jungles of Borneo that the natives had worshipped and called 'hantus' or ghosts. The hantus all had their heads twisted around backward.

I thought of Cynthia getting out of the shower and into my arms. Maybe she was wearing the little housecoat, maybe she wasn't. If she was, I had ways to make those parrots talk.

I thought of Gunner. I hadn't called her in weeks. The only hockey action she was likely to see this season might be a power play by me. Give her a couple of good body checks. Might slip one in her net if she wasn't careful.

I thought of Pete Myers, The Weasel, McGovern. I thought of myself. I looked at myself in the bar mirror, trying to keep my balance on the stool. I knew I wasn't as stupid as I looked. No one was. I let my eyes go out of focus so they could see what they wanted to see.

There were red lights blinking at me from the bar. It was the red neon bar sign that hung high above the sidewalk out in front of the place. It was reflecting on the rain-wet sidewalk and throwing double images at me through the mirror on the bar. And it was flashing the words EAR . . . BAR . . . EAR . . . BAR . . . EAR . . . BAR . . . right through my tequila-ized brain and out the other side. Suddenly I was sober as a judge. A warm wave rolled over me and I might even have smiled. I had it. I knew who the killer was.

Now if I could get someone other than the cat to believe me.

## 51

I was holding a postcard from Florida that the postman had just brought. It showed a beautiful girl in a little blue bikini walking along a sunny, sandy beach. The girl had a very nice bucket and it wasn't the kind you hold in your hand. Maybe if you knew her pretty well . . .

On the back of the postcard was a message from Cynthia. It read: 'Wish you were here. It's beautiful. Thanks for helping me through a hard time. Love, Cynthia. PS Coming home Tuesday night. Arriving at ten o'clock at La Guardia on Air Florida. I'm not an easy pickup but why not give it a try?'

Nina had called earlier that morning. She had finished working on the video and was wondering if I'd like to get together with her. Rambam called and wanted to know if I wished to go shooting with him. He didn't say shooting what and I didn't ask. My old friend Ted Mann called from California. He'd been in Hollywood for six months, writing movies to amuse Americans, and he was coming back this week. Wanted to go out and burp in the Indian restaurant where they had the sitar player. One of the things I could do was say the phrase 'I like Indian restaurants' in one belch. Ted said for me to round up McGovern and Boris and some of the boys.

'Might be a little difficult to get McGovern,' I told him.

'Why?' asked Ted.

'He's on a vacation,' I said.

'When's he coming back?' asked Ted.

'He's on a long vacation. We'll have to go to Indian restaurants without him for a while.'

No point in telling Ted yet. He'd find out soon enough. Everybody in New York except for him and the sitar player knew about McGovern already. And sometimes I wasn't so sure about the sitar player. He had a kind of smarmy, knowing look about him on occasion.

Brennan called and wanted to meet at the Monkey's Paw. Ratso called and wanted to meet at Big Wong's for lunch. Boris called and wanted to unload five pounds of caviar on me for a very reasonable price. Pete Myers finally called to express his sympathy about McGovern.

'Bit of hard luck, old man,' he said.

'Yeah.'

Even Dr Bock's office had called. The large secretary wanted to know why I hadn't paid the large bill.

It never fails. You're always in demand when you want to be alone.

I wound up spending the afternoon with the cat. There wasn't any rain so I couldn't watch it. The cat chased a few cockroaches and I chased my tail around the room waiting for Cynthia to get back the following night.

Maybe I truly missed McGovern. Maybe I was outraged at what I knew to be a thorough miscarriage of justice. Or maybe Ratso was right and my ego was just a little bruised from having Fox and Cooperman show me up so badly. Whatever it was, I wasn't quite through yet. I had one more card to play.

The monkey wasn't dead and the show wasn't over.

By 9.45 Tuesday night, Ratso and I were standing at the Air Florida baggage carousel at La Guardia Airport. He was wearing his coonskin cap without the tail and a black leather coat that was loaded to the gills with nonfunctional buckles and snaps.

'Don't fall asleep,' I said. 'Somebody might mistake you for their nice Italian luggage. You could wake up at the Hotel Pierre.'

'I could do worse,' he said.

We watched the carousel going round and round. It was completely empty except for a frilly, bright-red hatbox with a pink sash that looked like something Miss Kitty might carry in *Gunsmoke*. We watched it go around about twenty times.

'What comes around goes around,' said Ratso.

A frail, androgynous-looking young man came by, picked up the hat box, and stepped primly away with it.

'Not always,' I said. 'Life's full of little surprises. Sometimes God throws you a slider.'

I turned around and saw Cynthia coming down the walkway toward us. She was a vision and a half. Some girls shouldn't be allowed to go to Florida. I would always be a sucker for a suntan on a beautiful woman. I took a deep breath in spite of myself.

I thought of somebody else I'd gone to meet at an airport once. She was coming back from Mexico and I was coming back from

Mars. The girl was different of course. The times were different – it had been almost eight years ago. The airport had been in Los Angeles. Good old LAX.

The only things that were the same were the suntan and, I suppose, my heart.

'Oh, guys,' she said, 'what a sweet reception committee.'

'After what you've been through,' said Ratso, 'we couldn't do less.'

'You look great, Cynthia,' I said.

Ten minutes later we had the luggage stowed in the trunk and the three of us, with Cynthia in the middle, were rolling out of La Guardia in a Checker. 'Forty-two Jane Street,' Cynthia told the driver, 'in the Village.' We settled back for the ride.

We sped down the Grand Central Parkway to the Brooklyn-Queens Expressway, and when the Williamsburg Bridge, which would take us into the city, came into sight, I took a ragged piece of paper from the pocket of my coat. It was the napkin from the Carnegie Delicatessen.

'Have a look at this,' I said.

'Jesus,' said Ratso, 'not the old Carnegie Delicatessen Napkin Trick again.'

'He makes a good sandwich?' asked Cynthia. She laughed.

'Best pastrami in the city,' I said. 'Now I'd like to call your attention to the symbols on this napkin.' I showed them to Cynthia. I pointed out the first three initials:

C. . . . N. . . . M.

'This first is from the notes made by Frank Worthington's psychiatrist. It's my little "flow chart" and it shows the sequence of Worthington's relationships for what it's worth.

'Directly below we find another grouping of initials that an old girlfriend of Worthington's, Nina Kong, considered to be a more correct sequence. They are as follows:'

N. . . . C. . . . M.

I underlined the letters with my finger.

'Now the Rosetta Stone, it ain't. But it did fool us for a while.

You see, it doesn't really matter which version is the correct one. The point is that we always assumed the 'C.' stood for 'Campbell' as in 'Barry Campbell.' But what if, just for the hell of it, we say that the 'C.' stands for 'Cynthia,' as in 'Cynthia Floyd.' What if we say that you were once sadly, passionately, hopelessly, in love with Frank Worthington? I think you were. I think you were more than just in love with Frank Worthington. I think you wanted to *be* Frank Worthington.'

'What are you saying?' asked Cynthia.

'I'm saying I know you Sam Cooke'd him, baby,' I said.

'What is that supposed to mean?' she sniffed.

'You can look it up when you get home,' I said. I reached inside my hunting vest and pulled out a small parcel wrapped in an old page from the *Daily News*. I handed it to Cynthia. 'I got you a little present,' I said. 'Go ahead – open it.'

She put the package in her lap and tore off the newspaper wrapping. The three of us stared down at a frayed and fragile, worn and withered pink rose.

'I think it belongs to you,' I said. 'Kept it in the refrigerator for you.' Ratso looked at me, but Cynthia kept her eyes on the rose.

'Now cross-dressing and dressing identically can be a fun thing for a girl to do with her fella,' I said. 'But it gets to be a drag when the clothes start to make the man. Or the woman. And I do mean a drag.

'Watching her lover slowly evolve into a homosexual right before her eyes can't be much fun for a girl. It could even twist a girl's head around. But you carried the torch and you kept carrying it until that eternal flame burned your mind.

'Then one morning you walked down the hall and you saw the flowers that Barry Campbell, another man, had sent to Worthington on his birthday. The heat became too intense.

'You went to the *Daily News* as McGovern's girlfriend picking up some notes for him that he'd supposedly left at his desk. You typed your own little note at his typewriter. You returned home later, had a farewell drink with Frank, dispatched him to the happy homosexual hunting ground, left the card, took one flower, planted the receipt, and hid the gun in McGovern's apartment.

Later you sent the flower to me with another note you typed on McGovern's typewriter. Are you with me so far?'

Cynthia sat there like an autistic child but she had something in her eye and it wasn't the sort of thing that was ever going to be removed by a nice gentleman's handkerchief.

'Darlene Rigby was a problem,' I said. 'She'd inadvertently seen one thing she shouldn't have in her short life. The thing she saw was you and Frank Worthington together, possibly in your 'twin' get-ups. She was dying to tell me. But I made the mistake of mentioning it to you. Well, like it says on the wall above the bar at the Monkey's Paw, 'Loose lips sink ships.' Only you fixed it so that Darlene Rigby's whole goddamn harbor sank.

'I doubt if McGovern was onto you, but he did see a ghost. And the ghost was one of the things that drove him to turn himself in. You were the ghost, Cynthia – dressed as Frank Worthington. Just like the old days, right?

'Then, of course, you told the truth to the cops about overhearing McGovern's vague threats as he talked in his sleep. You couldn't tell a lie. But it gave you something to think about, and you used it that same night when you murdered Adrian. I congratulate you. It was very fast thinking and it was clever as all hell. Even more clever than using Worthington's voice on his old answering machine to scare the shit out of me and Ratso.

'You poisoned Adrian's Perrier, or was it the cocaine? The point is rather moot but, out of curiosity, which was it?'

Cynthia said nothing, but her eyes could have whipped up on somebody in the dart contest at the local pub.

'It doesn't matter,' I said. 'Say you cut Adrian's cocaine with something stronger than the Ajax she normally used. You came back later to check your handiwork. Now here is the clever part. I didn't get it myself until a couple of nights ago when I saw how the burned-out neon in a sign could change the word BAR to the word EAR. Anyway, as I was saying, you came back to check your handiwork and you saw that Adrian, in her death throes, had managed to write something in cocaine on the coffee table before she cashed in her chips. She'd written the word 'Cynthia.' The name of her killer.

'In a flash of diabolical brilliance, you, Cynthia, found a straw and snorted the little tail of the letter "y" in Cynthia, thereby changing the "y" to a "u." Then you Hoovered the 'hia' and that left only the word 'cunt' which would lead straight to McGovern once you told the cops what you'd heard him say earlier that night. The whole snorting operation must have given you quite a bit of satisfaction. Not to mention a little buzz.

'You killed two birds and got stoned. You snuffed Adrian who you thought was beginning to lamp you for what you were, and you put the final twist into the noose you knew would hang McGovern. But it won't, Cynthia. It'll allow me, instead, to tie up this whole unpleasant affair in a sailor's knot and hand it over to the police. I'm sure that Fox and Cooperman will be grateful for justice having been done, aren't you, Ratso?'

'Jesus,' said Ratso in a low voice.

Cynthia was laughing now. But her laughter sounded so canned you could almost taste the botulism breeding in it. Suddenly she stopped laughing. She spoke in a sweet, melodic voice. A little girl's voice.

'Perr-i-er,' she said. 'It was the Perr-i-er.'

A high keening noise emitted from her lips. It was the kind of sound you could only pray would end up on the cutting-room floor of your nightmares. Like listening to a hundred Arab women mourning in your Walkman.

Cynthia's eyes had now turned backward into her head. What she saw there God only knows. And he wasn't even clueing Moses.

I leaned forward and tapped on the partition of the cab.

'The lady looks sick, buddy,' the driver said. 'You want I should take her to a hospital?'

'Sixth Precinct, pal,' I said.

I took a last long look at Cynthia as we were coming down Seventh Avenue. The pink rose still lay in her lap like a languid lover. But all the color had drained completely from her face.

You can lose a tan pretty fast in New York.

## 52

'Sir, your coat's on the floor,' said the irritated young waitress in the little Greek coffee shop.

'Oh, thank you,' said McGovern.

'Just like old times,' I said. McGovern looked pretty good considering.

'I really feel like a chump,' said McGovern. 'She had such a nice, wholesome, innocent look about her. . . . When did you first suspect it was Cynthia?'

'Well, there were a number of little things that didn't quite ring true about her. Don't feel too bad about being a chump. I was taken in too. In a manner of speaking.

'When she came to visit me in the hospital, she was upset about your not trusting her more. Said it was partly her fault you were drinking and running from the cops and seeing ghosts in hallways. Now at that time, you still hadn't talked to her since you phoned her after finding Worthington's body. All you said to her was "Do you believe in ghosts?" That sounded pretty weird in itself when she told me about it. But the point is, you never told her about seeing ghosts in the hallways. 'How could she have known that?' I asked myself. There were only two possibilities. Either she'd seen the ghost in the hallway herself. Or – something I could hardly believe – she was the ghost in the hallway. Of course, the latter possibility was correct.

'Then I asked myself: "Who could have plausible access to your typewriter at the *Daily News*?" Who could have slipped the gun into your apartment undetected?' Cynthia had the means to do both, but I still couldn't be sure. So I borrowed a page from my old friend Sherlock Holmes, and I sent out a few telegrams to get a rundown on Cynthia's background. Her mother has had bouts with severe schizophrenia for years. Cynthia's mother's turbulent emotional history makes Zelda Fitzgerald look only as if maybe her guppies had died.

'For the past seven years her mother's been living in the monstro-wig ward of a Des Plaines, Illinois, mental hospital. And she ain't gettin' out soon.'

'Never knew a thing about it,' said McGovern. 'Cynthia never mentioned it.'

'It's not exactly the kind of thing she'd want to put in her résumé, but it does account for a great deal of Cynthia's bizarre, distorted, murderous frame of mind. Cynthia came by it honestly at least. Her father left home when Cynthia was very young. I understand he did a little time on the rock, too.'

'It's still hard to believe,' said McGovern.

'Well, I hate to be the one to take the flyswatter to Tinker Bell, but the girl was clearly a psychopathic liar, McGovern. And that was one of her more endearing qualities. She bullshitted me the first time I talked to her about how Adrian dropped off some cocaine for her. Adrian was pathological about not giving curb service. Many dealers are. Adrian wouldn't have brought it to you if you were standing in her kitchen.

'Then, after she'd croaked Adrian, Cynthia wanted some time to get her thoughts together. I tried for about two hours that night to get into the building and Cynthia pretended she wasn't there. When I called she said she'd just gotten out of the shower . . . She looked the part all right, but I remembered seeing my face in the bathroom mirror just before I went upstairs to find Adrian's body. Later I wondered, "How could I have seen my face in the mirror? Why wasn't it steamed?"

'You know the rest from what you've read and written in the papers. Cynthia'd waited a long time to take her revenge on Frank Worthington and you're a sweet, trusting kind of guy with a little bit of Gullible's Travels going for you. She just saw you coming and decided to hang her albatross around your neck.'

'She damn near did, too,' said McGovern.

'She felt she had to silence Darlene Rigby. She felt threatened by what she thought Adrian might have known, and being paranoid as all hell, she thought she had to silence her, too. No doubt about it. Cynthia was definitely cookin' on another planet, pal. I was probably next on her shopping list. We'll never know.'

'I'll buy you lunch,' said McGovern. 'I owe it to you. I hear you hada hole in your shoulder big enough to drive a truck through.'

'Maybe a Japanese import,' I said.

McGovern paid the cashier and we took a stroll through the Village. It was a cold afternoon but it was clear and sunny and we passed a pretty thing or two walking down Hudson.

We were almost to Jane Street when McGovern pulled up short at 634 Hudson. He pointed out a brand-new awning that read: MYERS OF KESWICK.

'I'll be damned,' I said. 'Pete Myers did it.'

'The place is a hit,' said McGovern. 'I come in here all the time. Pete's a very decent chap and the pork pies are the best in town.'

'They're also about the only ones in town,' I said, as we walked into the place. I had to admit the assortment of steak and kidney pies, Irish sausages, pork pies, and curried beef looked great even if you weren't British.

Pete was behind the counter. He came out and shook hands with us. 'Congratulations, Myers,' I said.

'And congratulations to you,' he said. 'You've beaten Scotland Yard again, Mr Holmes.' He laughed. He still had the same laugh. 'Can I help you lads?' he said.

'Yeah,' I said, 'I'll have a British Knish.'

'Would you believe,' said Myers, 'out of everything I make here, that was the only product that didn't sell.'

'Too bad,' I said. 'Seemed like a natural.' We bought a few pork pies from Myers, promised to be back again soon, and left the place.

'You see,' said McGovern, 'Myers is a straight arrow after all.'

'Don't wish that on anyone, McGovern,' I said. 'I think it's important for all of us to explore our bisexual feelings.'

'We don't have to do it right now, do we?' asked McGovern. The question did not dignify an answer so I didn't give it one. Instead, I looked back at the sign on the awning.

'Myers of Keswick,' I said. 'That's the place in England that all the poets are from, isn't it?'

'That's right,' said McGovern. 'I didn't know you knew that.'

'Oh, I know a lot of things, McGovern.'

'Do you know that the *w* in *Keswick* is silent?'

I was silent myself for a moment. Then I took out a cigar and fired it up. 'Goddamn Brits,' I said.

When we reached the old windmill across from his apartment, McGovern shook his head. 'Man, I'll tell you,' he said. 'That cocaine on the coffee table was a stroke of brilliance on your part.'

'It wasn't too shabby on Cynthia's part, either.'

'I still can't believe that Cynthia was capable of doing all that she did.'

'Oh, it's not so hard to believe,' I said. 'Just look up into the dark twisted limbs of that gnarly old family tree, pal. Blood will tell, McGovern. Blood will tell.'

'That's comforting,' said McGovern. He stood hesitating at the door of his building. 'You know,' he said, 'I'm almost afraid to go inside.'

'If you see another ghost in there, you're in trouble, pal,' I said.

## 53

It was a Tuesday evening or maybe it was a Thursday. It had been two weeks since we'd picked Cynthia up at the airport and nothing much was happening. The newspapers were already back to covering hit-run incidents, subway muggings, and child abuse. The usual stuff.

Ratso, the cat, and I had been just sitting around the loft looking at each other like three guests in a Roach Motel. I wandered over to the kitchen, picked up a bottle of Irish whiskey, and poured a long shot into the old bull horn. They say God created whiskey to keep the Irish from taking over the world. Maybe he created black-and-white TV to keep Ratso from taking over my couch. At any rate, Ratso was leaving.

'Wickedly clever. My hat's really off to you for solving this one. I never thought you would, to tell you the truth.'

'It's all in the wrist,' I said.

'I'll bet the cops never even thanked you.'

'Well, let's just say that all the publicity over the past two weeks hasn't exactly been brick and mortar to my relationship with Detective Sergeants Fox and Cooperman.'

'They'll get over it,' said Ratso. 'Look, Sherlock, I want you to take care of yourself. Stay away from The Weasel and his weasel dust. I know you're very vulnerable when you're between cases. I'll call you tomorrow.'

'Thanks, Rats,' I said. I let Ratso out, fed the cat, and sat back down at my desk waiting for the worm of happiness to turn my way. There are worse things in this world than being lonely, but I didn't ever want to find out what they were. I was used to lonely. Lonely fit me like an old hunting vest. I would wear it in good health.

I thought of McGovern. He was probably down at Costello's now, making up for a little lost time. Tomorrow morning Ratso would be back in his office taking meetings, goosing the secretary, going about the business of being an editor.

Calling Nina Kong wasn't in the cards. Three days before, I'd run into her, quite inadvertently, in the hallway of my building. I was taking out the trash and she was coming down from Winnie Katz's experimental dance class.

You can't win 'em all.

## 54

I got up one morning several weeks later feeling rested and optimistic about what the future might bring. The events of the past few months were well behind me. Cynthia was in some prison psycho ward where she belonged, all ghosts and doppelgängers had been banished, and my shoulder was about back to normal. I could shrug again.

I fed the cat, made some coffee, poured a cup, and stood at the kitchen window of the loft watching one of nature's greatest wonders, New York sunshine. I took out a handsome-looking, fresh cigar and was just starting to light it when the phones rang. I walked back to my desk where the phones were and noted it was 10.17 a.m. I lit the cigar. Never answer phones too quickly. Somebody might think you need work.

I took a puff or two on the cigar. The phones kept ringing. Being left-handed, I'd always had a little penchant for the phone on the left, but now I reached across and picked up the blower on the right. Thought I might diversify. Change my luck. Try something new.

'Start talkin',' I said.

The voice I heard was strange and disembodied, yet faintly, and frighteningly, familiar.

'This is Frank Worthington,' it said.

There was the sound of silence on the line and it wasn't the one by Simon and Garfunkel. Then I heard muffled laughter. It sounded like a squirrel or a rat. I couldn't be sure but I leaned toward the rat.

'Very cute, Ratso,' I said.

'It's heartening to see you haven't lost your powers of perception, Sherlock,' he said.

'Oh, it was very goddamn elementary, my dear Ratso,' I said. 'You bootlegged that tape from my loft.'

'Yeah, but how can you be so sure it was me?' Ratso shouted indignantly.

'Dead man's shoes,' I said.